Praise for *Landfall*

Welcome to your new favorite YA sci-fi series! *Landfall: The Ship Series Book One* hurls us into a frightening and fascinating future rich with action, mystery, and unforgettable characters. With elements of Orson Scott Card's Ender's Game and the best of Rick Riordan's Percy Jackson books, Landfall kept me burning through the pages. I hope Jerry Aubin is typing right now, because I can't wait to return to The Ship!

- Owen Egerton, author of *Everyone Says That at the End of the World*

HOMEWARD

THE SHIP SERIES // BOOK THREE

JERRY AUBIN

Text copyright © 2015 Jerry Aubin
Illustrations copyright © 2015 Jerry Aubin

For any information, please contact zax@theshipseries.com.

The main text of this book was set in Georgia.
The chapter title text was set in Avenir.

Lekanyane Publishing
Austin // Amsterdam // Cape Town // Sydney // Christchurch

ISBN 978-0-9970708-5-9 (pbk)
ISBN 978-0-9970708-4-2 (ebk)

For K, P, W, and Q.

CHAPTER ONE

This is the rock!

Markev's elbow accidentally poked his ribcage for the fifth time in the last thirty minutes. Adan responded by intentionally jamming his own into the giant man's beefy side.

"Why can't you manage to keep your body to yourself, you big oaf!"

"Sorry, sir. I think you should get your money back from whoever advertised this survey craft as fitting two people. Maybe you should've brought one of those puny engineers along for the ride instead of your bodyguard."

Adan grinned. "I thought about it, but unfortunately you're more intelligent than all of them combined. Still nowhere near as a smart as me, of course, but bright enough to be marginally useful."

"Thank you, sir. I guess." The man paused. "If I may—why is either one of us wasting time on this trip in the first place? You've got more money than most governments. Shouldn't you have just paid some prospector from the East to do all of this rock collecting for you?"

The frustration in Markev's voice was clear, and its source was understandable. They, along with a dozen engineers, had just completed their sixteenth month crammed into a spacecraft. Even though their main vessel was far larger than the tiny survey craft, the vast majority of its space was dedicated to supplies and fuel with very little volume remaining for living quarters. The human body wasn't designed to spend that amount of time crammed into impossibly small spaces. More importantly, the human mind wasn't designed to share those small spaces with other humans. This was especially true of Adan's own mind since he barely tolerated the existence of most other people under the best circumstances.

Markev was also correct about the ready availability of others to do the work. Miners from the East had traveled to the belt for decades and had made the journey itself routine, though primarily because they Uploaded all of their crews and passengers. For them, lengthy space travel experiences would be customized to whatever best suited the individual. More than one best-selling book had been written by people from the East who constructed a virtual desert island and then didn't interact with another living soul for the entirety of their voyage to the belt. As deeply as Adan believed Uploading one's mind and forfeiting one's physical body to be an abomination, sixteen months of breathing his own and other people's recycled farts had almost convinced him to rethink his position. Almost, but not quite. He replied.

"You really think I would outsource this particular project and then try to manage it from half a billion kilometers away? Haven't I made it abundantly clear how critical this effort is? Have you not been paying attention to how hands-on I've been with my most critically important projects?"

Adan had an even stronger justification, but he had to keep it hidden from everyone. He had accomplished something truly astounding with all of the isolated time during their journey, and his discovery would forever remove the vastness of space as a reason for people to abandon their bodies and Upload. He wasn't prepared to discuss it with anyone yet, not even Markev, but he was confident his results would stand up to scrutiny. Home was still at least a year away, and the return voyage would provide adequate time to re-validate his findings.

Markev still appeared dubious, but he nodded his head and then pointed to the viewscreen. "Here's our next candidate asteroid, sir. I can't believe we've been out here for four months, and this is only the seventh rock that's fit your search parameters. I always knew the belt was mostly empty space, but I never realized how much distance there was between its asteroids. This one measures one hundred kilometers long by fifty wide and ten thick, so it's smack in the sweet spot of your preferred dimensions. I've run the numbers and concluded we can also deorbit and redirect it toward home easily enough given the extra engines and fuel we're carrying."

Adan was excited the rock met their first two requirements regarding size and orbital plane. This wasn't the first time that had happened, though, and it was the final requirement where every other candidate asteroid had failed over the last few months—mineral composition. The East had spent a generation in the belt prospecting for those rare minerals that had the greatest value when shipped home. Adan wasn't searching for anything rare, however. Titanium wasn't valuable at home given its prevalence, but it was priceless when available as a building material in orbit. That was where his project would need an incomprehensible amount of it. There was only one way to find out whether this rock would meet their needs.

"Thanks, Markev. I'll deploy the core survey laser."

The device was his own brilliant design. It was responsible for the majority of his tremendous fortune thanks to all of the prospecting the East had done in the belt. Adan didn't like the East one bit and certainly didn't share their values, but he never let that get in the way of doing business with them. His laser had allowed them to harvest untold wealth from the belt, and

Adan's contracts with them had astutely called for ongoing mineral royalties rather than one-time payments.

The first pulse of the laser drilled the width of a human hair ten kilometers in the span of seconds. A second pulse performed laser spectroscopy along the entirety of the minuscule shaft to identify the mineral profile throughout the stratum. A couple of hours of work could create a detailed profile of any area being sampled, and Adan took the time necessary to evaluate the full width and length of the asteroid. His excitement level steadily increased until he eventually exclaimed his conclusion.

"This mineral profile couldn't be a better match. This is the rock!"

Markev had been staring at him worriedly, but the bodyguard's brow unfurrowed at Adan's words. "Finally. Shall I inform the rest of the crew?"

Adan shook his head. "Hold on. I need you to do something for me first. Vector us five kilometers above the surface."

Markev did as requested and Adan stared out the viewscreen with a widening grin. The asteroid below him had traveled the cold depths of space for billions of years. In a few short weeks it would have engines installed. It would cease to be a lifeless rock driven only by Newton's laws and instead be transformed into the most massive spacecraft ever envisioned. The engines were just the beginning, of course, and only temporary ones that would be used to manipulate the rock out of the belt and into orbit back home. That was when the real fun would start.

Hundreds of thousands of workers would swarm upon the asteroid once it arrived. The first phase would hollow out much of its interior to create massive agricultural and storage holds. The largest mining operation ever attempted in space would not only create those underground structures, it would also generate the building materials needed for phase two. Thousands of towering structures would next rise from the asteroid's surface. Adan's plans called for constructing what would be one of their world's largest metropolises but with an asteroid as its foundation. Rather than grow and evolve slowly over centuries, all of his city's structures would emerge simultaneously during a few frantic years.

A city traveling through the universe with millions of inhabitants—what a magnificent spaceship Adan was creating! This ship of his would need a name. An inspiring name would be the first critical step in the marketing campaign necessary to recruit a crew for its journey. Markev interrupted his reverie.

"What are you smiling about, sir?"

Adan pointed to his right and thirty degrees above the asteroid's surface. The faint blue dot with its ten billion inhabitants was exactly where he knew it would be.

"I can't wait to see what everyone back home on Earth thinks about our amazing new mission to save our species."

CHAPTER TWO

You totally deserve this.

K alare finished telling Zax her story about getting shot and being rescued by the Marines. She expected him to be happy to see her, but he appeared confused instead. He was an odd boy sometimes, and she never knew what was knocking around inside that skull of his. She was debating asking him to explain himself when the screens lit up around the mess hall to show the morning newsvid. She squealed in excitement.

"Ooohhh, we've got to watch this! There haven't been any broadcasts since everything happened, but I heard last night that we'd see a full report this morning about what ended the Revolution and how things are going to work around here now with the civilians in charge."

Kalare grabbed a chair and set it down next to Zax. She accidentally placed it too close to his but was too interested in what the announcer had to say to bother moving.

"We've got a special report for you today with the full details of what happened recently along with initial information about what you should expect to see moving forward.

"A group of brave civilians took decisive action three days ago based on concerns that have simmered this past year regarding the viability of our Mission. After evidence surfaced that additional humans are traveling the stars, these selfless individuals concluded they must influence a change in our Mission."

Kalare almost guffawed at the notion of civilians who had been "brave" enough to shoot a couple of unarmed cadets in the belly, but she remained silent.

"Their goal was to avoid as much bloodshed as possible while ensuring their message was heard and acted upon by the Captain and Omegas. They only took this action after repeated attempts at peaceful discussion through normal channels had been rebuffed. Thankfully, through the calm thinking of their leaders and the eventual cooperation of a senior member of the Crew, they were able to achieve their objectives."

A picture of the Boss popped up on the screen. He was bloodied and disheveled. Kalare marveled at how much torture the poor man must have endured in the name of protecting the Ship.

"The final resolution became possible when the Flight Boss determined he needed to step in to do what was best for everyone on the Ship—Crew and civilian alike. He was initially resistant to the requests of the civilians, as can be seen here with the physical evidence of how he withstood their augmented interrogation techniques. In an exclusive interview this morning, we learned the thought process behind how his conclusions shifted, and we will air that footage later. Suffice it to say, you'll want to hear it straight from his mouth.

"What I can tell you now is that the Boss realized the Captain's intent to vent the Ship and murder ten million humans was unjust and unlawful. He halted his resistance to the civilians' requests and ultimately brokered a deal between them and the Captain. This deal included the Captain's agreement to step down, temporarily, pending a full review of her actions. The Flight Boss is now in charge of all Crew matters, albeit within a new command structure that includes much needed civilian oversight. It is this new leadership structure that we are going to discuss first, starting with this footage from an announcement that was made earlier this morning."

Zax bolted upright. "That's entirely a lie! None of that happened like what they're saying! The Boss wasn't tortured, he didn't broker any deal, he just gave in to the civilians plain and simple and sold out the

Captain in the process. All to save his own skin and stay in charge!"

Zax's sudden movement surprised Kalare, and she sat up straight with momentary alarm. She listened to his outburst, paused for a moment, then leaned back and slowly shook her head and sighed. "Not this all over again. Didn't you learn your lesson the last time you went looking for imaginary conspiracies involving the Boss?"

Zax stared at her with fire in his eyes. Kalare met his gaze and didn't flinch. Thirty secs later, he finally broke eye contact. "You're right. I'm an idiot. I think the pain meds have me feeling wonky. I'm sorry."

Kalare didn't believe he was being genuine, but he had been through a lot over the past few days and she didn't want to add to his stress. She was dying to learn what happened with Zax and the Boss right before the civilians took over that had him so worked up, but everything about his tone and body language suggested this wasn't the time. She changed the topic instead.

"Do you have any clue what your duty assignment is going to be? They wouldn't send you back to Waste Systems after all you've done, would they? No way they would. At least, I wouldn't if I was in charge. Imagine what things would be like if I were in charge? I hope I wouldn't have made some of the same choices the Captain just made that got us into this whole mess in the first place. Imagine that...Captain Kalare. It has a pretty nice ring to it, don't you think?"

Zax paused for a deep breath before speaking. He did that a lot, and Kalare never quite understood what was behind it.

"No, I'm not going back to Waste Systems. Like you predicted, the Boss rewarded me for everything I did to keep him out of the hands of the civilians. I'll be in Flight Ops once they finish getting it up and running again. I'm also entering the Pilot Academy."

Zax was downplaying the news for some reason, but his excitement was obvious to Kalare. It was excitement she genuinely shared.

"Wow, Zax, that's awesome! I'm so happy for you. You totally deserve this. I'm thrilled we'll be working together again. I'm even more excited we'll be in the Academy at the same time! The way they do the training we'll still see each other a lot even with me a year ahead. Maybe I'll even get to do some of your instruction!"

"Thanks. It would be great if you did some of my training. I'm really excited about us spending a lot more time together as well."

Zax punctuated his last statement with an odd smile. Kalare was at a loss as to what the expression might mean, but for some reason it made her slightly uncomfortable. She stood to leave.

"I've got to get going. I told Captain Clueless I'd visit him in medbay after I had a chance to catch up with you. I can't believe he isn't up and about yet. We both got shot in the belly, and yet here I am all fine. He keeps whining about how his spine got nicked, but I think he's just malingering so he doesn't have to help with the cleanup around the Ship."

The mention of Aleron changed the expression on Zax's face. The odd smile was replaced with a tight grimace.

"When did you two become such buddies?"

"With all of the wounded, they doubled us up during our recovery. We didn't have anything else to do, so we got to chatting. I'm not trying to diminish how much he's tormented you, Zax, but he doesn't really seem like that bad of a guy. Maybe picking on you was all just the influence of that idiot mentor of his."

Zax's grimace transformed into a tight smile, but once again Kalare wasn't convinced he was being genuine. His flat tone served to reinforce her suspicions, even if his actual words tried to suggest otherwise.

"Maybe you're right. I'm glad you two are getting along so well. I should get going too. I don't have much time to prepare for my first day at the Academy."

"Prepare? I just showed up on my first day and jumped right in."

Zax smiled, genuinely this time, as he shook his head and stood up.

"There's that fantastic Kalare approach to her career that never ceases to boggle my mind. I'm so happy you're alive. I don't know what I would have done without you around."

"Me too! I'll see you later, Zax. The Boss has me running around like crazy today, but let's meet here again tomorrow morning."

CHAPTER THREE

You led a Revolution, you won, and now you're in

charge.

The small meeting room was jammed to bursting with both key civilians and senior members of the Crew. Imair had intentionally picked a room that was too small for the group she had called together. Forcing people into close proximity was a good way to accelerate the team-building process, which she knew would be critical to their ultimate success. She was not foolish enough to believe the Crew would truly accept their new civilian co-workers as teammates only six days after their world had been upended, but she had to start breaking down barriers as fast as possible to maintain the fragile peace on the Ship.

Madam President. Imair rolled the title around in her head. The Ship had been under military command for 5,000 years, so the notion of a civilian president with final authority would take significant time for everyone to accept. It wasn't without precedent in human history, however. Imair had devoured the Ship's history texts and learned that many nations of ancient Earth were organized such that an elected civilian was the Commander-in-Chief of their military forces.

Imair's position, though, did not come from the will of the people through any form of election. Her claim to power was based upon a pile of explosives that now ringed the Ship's Faster-Than-Light drive. The badge on her chest was actually a detonator that would allow her, or any of her most trusted lieutenants who wore similar devices, to initiate the destruction of the most irreplaceable piece of equipment on the Ship. Without a functional FTL drive, they would be effectively stranded for all eternity. Yes, the Ship was still capable of travel at near-light speed, but they would run out of fuel and other critical resources long before they reached a habitable planet.

Imair had pulled the Flight Boss aside yesterday, demonstrated how the badges worked, and explained how they had been distributed among the senior civilians. The man had blanched at the notion of any single person having the power to maroon the Ship—either intentionally or accidentally. Imair had ensured proper safeguards were in place to prevent any unauthorized or accidental initiation of the destruction sequence, but she didn't bother to share this fact with the Boss. A little fear and uncertainty would likely prove useful in keeping the Omega in line.

The Boss sat off to the side and stared at Imair as he waited for her to start the meeting. The impassive demeanor he tried to exude was betrayed by the tightness of his jaw muscles as he chewed one of his ever-present cigars. If by some miracle they worked together long enough to trust one another, Imair would have to inform the man of this behavioral "tell" to help him do a better job keeping his thoughts and emotions hidden.

The attendees were almost perfectly split between civilians and Crew. Imair had hoped there might be some amount of accidental integration, but that hadn't happened. The room was bisected with Crew on the right and civilians on the left. Multiple people on both sides had even chosen to stand rather than occupy the lone empty chair that divided the two factions.

Imair cleared her throat loudly. After a couple of secs the various discussions around the compartment ceased, and all eyes fell on her. She'd already been involved in smaller group conversations with almost everyone present, but this was her first time to address the new leadership "team" in its entirety.

"Good morning. It's great to see everyone together at last. Even better to see the degree of unity exhibited in how the two groups have arranged yourselves around the room."

There were a few tentative smiles and a couple of nervous titters in response to Imair's attempt at dispelling some of the tension in the room with sarcasm. Only Rege broke into prolonged laughter, and his manic tone was such that it was putting everyone else on edge rather than easing any apprehension. Imair needed to keep a close eye on him. All of the civilians came to this fight with well-earned anger over how they had been treated their entire lives, but she feared that Rege had the potential to cross over the thin boundary that separates freedom fighter from sociopath. He was too valuable a resource and had established too many deep relationships throughout the ranks of the Revolution to try to marginalize him right away. Nonetheless, she needed to monitor him and consider how to safely remove him from the equation.

"My apologies for leading off with a bad joke in these trying times. I know there has been a lot of change to digest. I also know that all of us lost friends and colleagues during the recent events." A smirk formed around the cigar in the Boss's mouth. Imair paused for a moment. "Is there something you would like to say, Boss?"

"Excuse me, *Madam President*, but I was reacting to your use of the phrase 'the recent events.' The victors get to write the history, so I'm sure some civilian years in the future will soften how he describes what happened here. I would respectfully suggest, however, that you own your actions and call them what they were. Revolution. You led a Revolution, you won, and now you're in charge. Calling a thing by its proper name isn't going to make us in the Crew feel any worse about it, but trying to dance around it with euphemisms most certainly will. Ma'am."

Everyone on both sides held their breath while they waited for Imair's response.

"Thank you, Boss. I deeply appreciate and value that direct feedback." Imair turned her gaze around the room and made eye contact with everyone in it while she delivered her next point. "Each of you should feel empowered to provide the type of constructive input the Boss just did. It's going to be a long time before everyone in this room can truly trust each other, but the only way we're going to keep this Ship safe going forward is if we get to that point sooner rather than later. Being able to speak our minds without fear of repercussions is a critical part of how that will happen. Understood?"

"Yes, ma'am."

The affirmative response wasn't universal and didn't convey nearly the enthusiasm Imair would have liked, but it was sufficient for this first meeting. She pushed ahead.

"The days since *the Revolution* have been filled with the most urgent tasks to help our wounded, mourn our dead, and triage the damage to the Ship. Everyone here has pulled double-shifts and operated on limited sleep to make this happen. You've all done amazing work, and I want to offer my heartfelt thanks.

"We must now enter a new phase. I ask each of you to work even harder in the weeks ahead. You've done admirably well at cleaning up after the Revolution, but now we have to build for what comes next. The future of this Ship is to return to its past— we're going to retrace our steps and visit the colonies we've established to search for the other humans we know are traveling the stars. This shouldn't be a random journey but instead one that has been thought out and designed to provide the best odds of crossing paths with our fellow travelers."

The civilians gave the impression of being uniformly excited while the Crew were almost uniformly dubious—the Boss being the only one who reacted like he was buying into her plan. Imair didn't have time to concern herself right now with whether his reaction was legitimate or an act, but it bore careful observation going forwards. She finished up her words for the group.

"It should be clear for each of you what needs to be done to prepare for what's next. If it isn't, please find me and let's discuss. We'll convene again in this room in exactly two weeks to discuss the plan in detail and ensure we all agree about how we're moving forward. You're all dismissed with the exception of the Boss and Rege."

After everyone filed out, Imair turned to the Boss.

"I meant it when I said I appreciated your candor earlier, Boss. Please keep it up. I trust you'll be a great role model in helping others understand this is not a dictatorship where I want to hear nothing but 'yes' all of the time. If we can't work together to come to the best possible solutions, then we have zero chance of success. Thank you."

The Boss kept his expression neutral but nodded his head in acknowledgement. Imair continued.

"There is one final loose end we need to take care of. I'd like the three of us to head over to the brig."

The Boss stood before he spoke. "With all due respect, Madam President, I will take care of this on my own. I don't think either of you have anything worthwhile to add to the process. Permission to be dismissed?"

Imair stared at the Boss for a dozen secs, but his expression remained impassive. She turned to Rege, who gave an almost imperceptible nod, and then back to the Boss.

"Dismissed, with the understanding Rege and I will instead be watching via the observation cameras."

The Boss nodded. "By all means."

CHAPTER FOUR

This doesn't feel right, Boss.

The Boss entered the brig and located the cell he wanted. He dismissed the guard with instructions he was not to be disturbed. As he sat down at the observation station outside the cell, an icon blinked to signify that video and sound were being transmitted elsewhere. The Boss couldn't care less if Imair and her stooges observed remotely, but he sure as hell wasn't going to let them be present.

The cell was intentionally barren with its only contents being a titanium bunk affixed to the deck and a toilet made of the same material with a lid that sealed tight when not in use. As the Boss sat down, the Captain rose from her bunk and leaned against the bulkhead nearest the toilet. Her expression was blank as she stared at him through the transparent titanium. Finally, she spoke.

"Saw your little performance on the newsvid. Someone did a great makeup job to get you looking all tortured up like that. But look at you now—not a mark on you. You couldn't be bothered to keep up the charade and sport some fake bruises for a few more days? You don't seriously trust the civilians to keep the truth to themselves, do you?"

"What does it matter, ma'am? It's not like anyone from the Crew pays attention to anything the civilians say. I can't fault you for being upset about the situation we're in, but do you honestly believe you'd be doing anything different if our positions were reversed?"

"I don't know, Boss, I just don't know. Perhaps you can help me understand your decision a little better to make it easier for me to empathize with you. From where I sit, I was about to enact the contingency plan that numerous other captains have triggered in the past. An action that all of us Omegas understand may be required of us to protect the Mission. Venting the Ship is clearly an option of last resort, and I was doing it only upon tremendous deliberation. If you think you wouldn't make that choice yourself to prevent the civilians from taking over, then when the hell else would you?"

The Captain knew how this conversation would end. She wasn't arguing and there was no malice in her eyes as she spoke. She was genuinely curious. The Boss didn't want to drag the ordeal out any longer than he had to, but he owed her at least some measure of closure.

"I understand, Captain. I really do. If I had been in your position on the Bridge, I would have issued that order as well. All of us Omegas would have. That's why Alpha took action and recommended that I enact Order Sixty-Six. A captain last vented the Ship a thousand years ago, and a lot has changed since then. You know as well as I do that we're approaching the point of collapse. We barely keep ahead of the critical maintenance that sustains operational readiness. Alpha projected that the shock of a venting plus the effort involved in the subsequent repopulation would have finally destroyed our ability to continue the Mission. I agreed."

The Captain listened intently and nodded along, but suddenly she stopped short and her eyes went wide.

"Wait—did you say that Alpha instigated Order Sixty-Six?"

"Yes, ma'am."

The Captain remained silent for a few long beats. She slowly shook her head when she spoke.

"This doesn't feel right, Boss. For obvious reasons the usage of Order Sixty-Six is something that all captains study to be sure we avoid those same mistakes. There are no records of the order ever being instigated by Alpha. Every single instance in history began with an Omega or group of Omegas who approached Alpha and argued the case for a captain's removal. Doesn't that strike you as odd that Alpha would act differently now?"

The Boss was only partially paying attention to the Captain's words. She had earned closure, but not the right to tie him up all day. While she spoke he maintained eye contact out of politeness but keyed the necessary authorization codes into the console. A red button lit up in response and slowly flashed next to his right hand. He casually moved that hand toward the button and hovered his index finger over it. When the Captain ended her observations with a question, it forced him to focus and mentally replay the conversation.

The Boss hesitated once he processed and understood the potential impact of her words. The icon continued to blink, and he considered the civilians who were watching his every move. The Captain's fate was sealed. Engaging in any further discussion would only risk information coming to light that he might regret Imair learning. The time for talking was past. It was time for action.

"This would have been an interesting philosophical conversation over drinks, ma'am, but we both know that can never happen now. I'm sorry."

Unlike most prisoners who wound up in this cell, the Captain was well familiar with its design and knew what was coming next. Before the final words left the Boss's mouth she dropped to the deck and threw her arms around the base of the toilet. Her right hand clutched her left wrist as the Boss's finger came down and the button stopped flashing and lit solid amber.

What appeared to be a solid bulkhead opposite the observation station was instead an exterior hatch that flew open and exposed the Captain to the vacuum of space. Even though the decompression was swift and violent, the cell contained a limited amount of atmosphere and the venting lasted for only a sec or two. The Captain's muscles and veins bulged mightily during that short time, but her grip held and her arms eventually went slack once the pressure was equalized.

The Boss swore under his breath once it became clear what the Captain had accomplished. Of course the ultimate outcome wouldn't be any different, but she was drawing the process out as long as possible. He met her gaze as she slowly expelled the air in her lungs. It was counterintuitive to discard precious oxygen if you found yourself exposed to a vacuum, but all Crew knew the risk of having your lungs rupture if you didn't release some of their relatively high pressure contents. The Boss refused to look away. The time in which the Captain would stay lucid was measured in secs, and she would be denied the satisfaction of seeing his frustration at her final stunt.

The Captain remained impressively stoic even as blood vessels burst in the whites of her eyes and a spurt of blood escaped her nose and instantly froze. Though her eyes remained open throughout, within a min they had become vacant and she was clearly no longer conscious. Had he any reason to do so, the Boss could seal the compartment and the Captain could be revived and suffer no lingering effects. That was not going to happen. Instead, he stared into her increasingly lifeless eyes until the cell's biomonitors chimed and signaled she was dead.

The Boss closed the exterior hatch and restored atmosphere to the cell. He considered leaving the body for someone else to deal with but then chose to finish what he started. He entered the cell and withstood the urge to gag at the smell of voided bowels. He removed the Captain's arms from around the toilet and positioned her body against the exterior hatch. The blue tint to her skin from the lack of oxygen made the scar on her throat even more pronounced than usual. The Boss reached over and attempted to close the woman's eyes, but they were frozen open. She deserved better, but that made her just like the rest of the Crew who deserved far better than the civilian rule they were now stuck with.

Once the cell was sealed tight behind him, the Boss increased the pressure within it to twice the normal setting. There would be zero doubt about the Captain's corpse being blown well clear of the Ship this time. He keyed his authorization code once more, and when he pressed the button everything worked as expected. The Boss stood and presented a mock salute to the camera which was still broadcasting to Imair.

CHAPTER FIVE

Half.

Zax's first day in the Pilot academy began with emotional extremes. Breakfast started on a high note when he scored the last of his favorite pastries. Even though there continued to be plenty of food in the mess hall since the civilian uprising, there had been spotty availability of certain items including the sweet he enjoyed the most.

His short-lived positive energy suffered a killing blow when Zax received a message via his Plug as he sat down. Kalare was supposed to be there for their typical morning meet up, but was skipping breakfast because "Aleron asked for some help with something." Kalare had spoken the name of his long-time nemesis far, far too often over the past few days. He attempted to rationalize it away as a short-term blip given their shared experience at the hands of the civilians, but his only friend talking repeatedly about the boy Zax despised was pushing him to his breaking point.

Zax struggled to decipher his uncomfortable mixture of feelings about Kalare's message until he got distracted. The morning newsvid had started, and an image of the Captain pushed Kalare out of his mind.

"I'm sad to report the Captain was discovered dead in her cell yesterday. She left behind a suicide note that expressed deep remorse for her personal treatment of the civilians and took full responsibility for forcing them into taking their recent drastic actions. She concluded her farewell message by requesting that everyone in the Crew learn from her mistakes and focus on working side-by-side with the civilians for the good of the Ship and the ultimate survival of all humanity."

The announcer paused as if he was dealing with some form of internal debate. He looked quickly at someone off-camera and then took a deep breath before addressing the audience again.

"She was a fine captain and will be missed by all of us who understood her contributions to our Mission."

The Captain's days were numbered based on the conversation Zax had witnessed between her and the Boss during the civilian uprising, but he was shocked to learn she was dead by her own hand. It was even more surprising to learn that she apologized to the civilians. The fact the civilians were treated poorly was clear to Zax, but it didn't ring true the Captain would see things the same way—much less feel remorse about the situation. Zax wanted to talk through the situation with Kalare when he saw her, though her reaction the last time he tried to share his doubts about something from the newsvid had not ended well. It was most likely moot. Given how much time she was spending with that oxygen thief, he'd probably never see Kalare again anyway.

Zax's stomach churned once more at the thought of Kalare and Aleron together, so he gave up on breakfast to make his way to the Pilot Academy instead. He cleared away his tray with all of its uneaten food and headed to the mess hall exit. Rege was entering, but the civilian was talking with someone else and Zax avoided being seen by him. Flight Ops wasn't operational yet, so Zax had not been forced to spend any additional time with the deranged civilian. That good luck was about to expire, though, since duty shifts there were rumored to begin the day after next.

The Tube wasn't reconfigured to allow civilians to ride yet, so it had been shut down until that work was complete. *In the interest of fairness to all.* Forcing the Crew to walk for no good reason was a colossal waste of everyone's time, but Zax put his fifteen mins journey to good use. He pushed the visions of Kalare and Aleron laughing together out of his mind and replaced them with excited thoughts about what training would be like in the Academy.

Zax arrived ten mins early and was underwhelmed. So much of the Ship that was dedicated to Flight involved environments that were impressive—Flight Ops with its massive, dual panoramas, the sheer volume of the hangar—that Zax had imagined the Academy to be a shining pilot factory. The first room he encountered was nothing but a dingy meeting space like so many others on the Ship. It held ten rows of ten seats arranged amphitheater style around a lectern. Zax picked a spot up front and observed as the room filled in.

The vast majority of the arriving cadets had been in Theta Cadre for the past year along with Zax, so he recognized their faces and the names on their uniforms even though he had rarely, if ever, interacted with them. Zax had worried he'd stand out as the oldest cadet since most enter the Academy during year one of Theta, but there were more than a few cadets sprinkled throughout the compartment who were most likely even older. On the other end of the age spectrum, one cadet was clearly young enough to still be in Zeta or Epsilon. He stood a quarter meter shorter than Zax and his head was shaved practically to the scalp with just the slightest hint of light blond fuzz. The boy sat down next to him, and Zax snuck a peak at the name on his uniform. If Mase was indeed as young as he appeared, then he must be pretty talented to be entering the Academy so early. Or he had a particularly influential mentor. Either way, he was someone worth keeping an eye on.

The background chatter hushed as a woman entered the compartment and walked down to the lectern. She was extremely tall—more than two meters—and carried her height with posture and grace that accentuated her near perfect physical conditioning. Thick and glossy chestnut hair framed an oval face with the palest green eyes Zax had ever seen. The woman's uniform featured a patch with a pair of wings superimposed on a starfield, and this identified her as a pilot. She surveyed the cadets before her for a few secs with a neutral expression.

"Good morning. My name is Major Eryn, and I have led the Pilot Academy for the last twenty years."

The major was either far older than her appearance suggested, or she had been promoted at an absurdly young age. Zax assumed it was the latter. She continued.

"All of you here today represent the best the Ship has to offer. You rank at or near the top of your cadres' Leaderboards and have sponsors and mentors who have staked their reputations on your nomination to enter. The majority of you come from Theta Cadre, but we also have a handful of aspiring pilots getting a late start out of Kappa Cadre. I particularly admire our oldest cadets who are starting their second year in Kappa. If they remain enrolled until their training is complete in two years, they will have chosen to spend an extra year as a cadet. Now that's dedication."

The major paused for a moment before looking toward Zax. He squirmed at the prospect she might call attention to his being at the very top of the Theta Leaderboard. Or perhaps mention his role in keeping the Boss safe during the Revolution.

"Most impressively, for the first time in over a decade, we have an exceptionally young cadet in our midst. One who was selected for the Academy during his first year in Zeta Cadre. He has set a new record on the Zeta Leaderboard with a score nearly double that of his nearest rival."

Everyone around the room craned their necks to follow the major's eyes as they focused on the boy next to Zax. Mase kept his eyes locked on the woman, and his expression didn't change despite all of the attention directed his way. Pretty impressive composure for a fourteen-year-old cadet. As much as Zax had worried about receiving any special attention from the major, he was stung by a sharp pang of jealousy when she instead praised the boy.

"We have one last housekeeping item before we get started. I want you all to count off alternating between one and two. Let's start with the cadet here in the first seat."

The major pointed at Zax who replied with a loud "one." Mase followed with a "two" and the remaining cadets repeated the pattern around the room until all one hundred had spoken.

"I'm pleased we managed to do that without any issues or confusion. Every few years a class manages to screw up that simple exercise, and more often than not it's a signal they'll continue to frustrate me over the entirety of their two-year term.

"I want all of my ones to look to your right and all of my twos to look to your left. The person next to you will be your training partner for the next month. This first pairing will only last a month because we will drop the two lowest ranked cadets from the program at the end of that time and then rearrange the pairings. This process of dropping cadets and rearranging the pairings will continue for the next two years, at which point I will graduate exactly half of you who are here today. Half." The major paused to let the word sink in. "Between the two of you who are looking at each other right now, odds are that only one will become a pilot. I suggest you give your partner a good once over and ask yourself how you'll beat him or her out for that spot."

Given a nearly unhealthy obsession with worst-case scenarios, Zax had never been one to suffer from overconfidence. Nonetheless, he often looked around and convinced himself he was the smartest cadet involved with any given activity. Mase, who sat and stared back at him with an expression devoid of any emotion, was likely destined to hold that top spot in their Academy class. At the age of fourteen no less!

Zax allowed himself a smile. He would not waste any mental energy figuring out how to win against the boy genius but instead focus on identifying the fifty other cadets he would beat out. He had worked too hard for too long and suffered too much for anyone to get in the way of his wings.

CHAPTER SIX

We are heading back the way we came.

H is first two days in the Pilot Academy left Zax as bored as the worst parts of his previous cadet training. The sessions were nothing but his fellow cadets asking stupid questions and then getting berated by instructors. Even though the introductory material was clearly a challenge for some of his classmates, Zax had spent so much time studying orbital mechanics while he built his fighter sim that he fought to remain awake. The sole bright spot was identifying a handful of cadets who were undoubtedly among the first to get booted from the Academy. He was safe from Major Eryn's cadet dismissals for at least the first few months.

Zax filled his tray with the usual breakfast assortment, including two of his favorite pastries, and spotted Kalare. She wasn't at their usual table because a group of civilians was sitting there instead. At least Rege wasn't with them.

"Good morning, Zax. How're you doing? How were the first few days in the Pilot Academy? I saw your class from across the hangar yesterday when you were getting your tour. I wanted to run over and say hello, but I was with Major Eryn and she doesn't appreciate it when I do things like that."

Zax grinned at the vision of Kalare interacting with the major. The Omega running the academy had come across as fairly icy and unlikely to appreciate Kalare's particular brand of exuberance.

"It's been OK. All of this intro material is stuff I already know, but it's letting me get a jump on what's coming next. About halfway through the first-year syllabus, I've run into topics that I haven't been exposed to before, so I'm doing some background reading to get ready for those."

"There's a syllabus? Cool! How come I've never seen that? They must not have had one for my class. It would've been interesting to know what was coming up, though I don't think I would've done anything differently with that information."

Zax wanted to laugh at Kalare's notion his was the first year where they created a syllabus. In fact, the changelog on the document showed it had not been updated in almost twenty years. As always on the Ship, once they found something that worked they tended to stick with it. How someone who never managed to plan beyond her next meal managed to stay so close to him on the Leaderboard would forever be one of life's great mysteries. Zax changed the subject.

"You should see this Mase kid I'm partnered with. He's only fourteen! He barely ever opens his mouth, but it's clear he knows even more than I do about all the stuff we're looking at. In fact, he corrected the woman leading a session yesterday afternoon. He jumped in and pointed out one of her orbital calculations was off by a thousandth of a percent. You know I'm not one for random chitchat, but this kid's silence makes me look practically like...well...like you."

"Everyone in my class is talking about him as well! They're all trying to figure out good ways to trip him up and take him down a few notches when we get a chance to lead some of the training for you guys. Doesn't strike me as being worth the energy. It's not like we're competing for the same slots or anything, so I don't get why anyone in my class feels it necessary to go after some kid in yours. It's such a funny coincidence that your first partner in the Academy doesn't talk much. My first partner didn't either! Come to think of it, I've had a whole string of partners who were pretty quiet."

Zax refused to touch that comment. Too, too easy.

"What can you tell me about Major Eryn? We haven't seen too much of her yet."

"You're going to like her, Zax. She's super, super smart. She's pretty tough as well. When we did some hand-to-hand combat training a few months ago, she stepped in to lead the class when the instructor got hurt. She's not Mikedo-level badass, but she's close."

A pang of sorrow arose at Kalare's mention of Mikedo, but all the craziness of the last week had pushed those old emotions pretty deep and Zax moved past it quickly. Kalare continued.

"She's pretty focused on the big picture, so it's great to not have all of the little, annoying demerits that many instructors enjoy doling out. Don't cross her, though. She hit one of the cadets in my class with 30,000 demerits a few months ago. I never heard the full story about what happened, but clearly she will do more than just boot you out of the Pilot Academy if you give her reason."

Zax had no intention of doing anything to anger the major, but he made note of the story to learn more about what happened. A message arrived via his Plug that made Zax groan.

"Are you seeing this too?"

"Yeah," replied Kalare. "Too bad Flight Ops isn't ready yet. I'm not that shocked based on the images of the damage we saw, but I was excited about getting back in there today. I wonder what we're going to talk about during this meeting the Boss has called instead."

"I don't know." Zax stood and grabbed his empty tray. "We should get going, though. I don't want to risk being late for my first interaction with the man in a week."

Their trip between the mess hall and Flight Ops was uneventful, though Zax swore there were far more civilians roaming the halls than he had seen previously. Were all of these people actually around for official business, or were they just taking advantage of newfound freedom to explore areas of the Ship they hadn't seen previously? Either way, it gave the passageways a vibrancy that Zax didn't believe had existed when he last roamed this part of the Ship a year ago.

They passed the entrance to Flight Ops while a group of maintenance staff happened to be leaving. Kalare snuck a quick glance inside and then smiled at Zax.

"It's pretty close to being ready. Everything is so new and shiny!"

Zax wanted to be excited about a refurbished Flight Ops. He had a hard time putting aside the knowledge that a week ago the compartment had been shredded by explosives and covered with the shattered remains of Crew and civilians. He was still trying to reconcile his feelings when they reached the conference room.

The Flight Boss sat on a table near the entrance, and Zax involuntarily paused for a moment. They were supposed to have met right after Zax got out of medbay, but the Boss cancelled at the last moment. This was his first encounter with the Omega since the man restored Zax's career with his award of 50,000 credits following the Revolution. The officer turned toward Zax and what might have been a genuine smile formed around the man's cigar.

"It's good to see you, Zax. It was unfortunate I had to cancel on you the other day, but my new boss can be a bit of a..." The Boss paused and glanced at three civilians who sat nearby. "Well, let's just say that I'm still getting used to the situation. How's the Pilot Academy?"

Zax had mentally prepared for this first meeting, but his legs still wobbled in the man's presence. There was an uncomfortably long pause as Zax calmed his body and gathered his wits.

"It's fine, sir. A little boring right now given I've already studied a lot of the initial material, but I'm confident it's going to be a wonderful experience."

"I heard you got partnered up with that fourteen-year-old from Zeta. I still can't believe Major Eryn lobbied so hard for him to get in at his age. The only reason the rest of us approved it was because she's been mentoring the boy for a while and acknowledged her career was on the line. I suggest you keep that relationship in mind during your dealings with him, Zax. You understand what I'm getting at?"

"Yes, sir."

That explained how Mase qualified to enter the Academy so young. Of course, it would be wildly hypocritical of Zax to fault Mase for taking advantage of an influential mentor and getting into the Academy. If anything, he had new appreciation for the pressure the boy must be under. Having a mentor put her career on the line in your name was stressful enough, but that pressure must be significantly compounded for Mase by having to toil under the major's direct oversight. The Boss was right—that relationship deserved careful observation as long as Mase and Zax were competing against each other.

The Boss looked back and forth at Zax and Kalare. "It will be good to have the two of you working for me together again. Go ahead and grab a seat. We're about to start."

They settled in and two mins later the Boss rapped his knuckles on the table to get everyone's attention. The room went silent and all eyes focused forward on the Omega.

"Good morning, everyone. It's unfortunate that we are having this first meeting here instead of Flight Ops. Maintenance has assured me they are completing the final items and will be ready for us tomorrow. I want to give you—"

The Boss was interrupted by Rege walking through the hatch. Zax's stomach clenched at the sight. The civilian must have fallen back into his old grooming habits since Zax had last seen him, as the man's hair was once again as stringy and unwashed as it was the day of the Revolution.

The Boss clearly fumed about Rege's tardiness and the interruption it caused, but the civilian acted oblivious as he greeted a few of the other civilians present and made his way to an empty seat alongside them. The Omega took a deep breath and continued.

"As I was saying, I want to provide an initial briefing on what's going to happen next. Plans are not yet complete, but they will be within a few days. Here's what I know.

"We're heading back the way we came to visit a sample of the colonies we've established. Our goal is to find additional traces of the other humans we believe are out here based on evidence that was discovered last year."

The Boss glanced in his direction and Zax averted his gaze rather than meet the man's eyes. It was a quick enough exchange that no one should have noticed, but Rege stared at him from the other side of the room. Zax focused on the Boss's words again.

"Our exact course is not yet final, but initial expectations are that we'll visit our first colony in six months. The rules of engagement with the colonists when we visit will be simple—we will not engage. The people we left on these colonies are no longer on board the Ship for a reason. There's no purpose in reconnecting with them only to abandon them a short time later. We'll use stealth drones to evaluate the condition of each colony and explore their planet for any clues about our fellow space travelers. If we see anything worth investigating further, we'll send small expeditions instructed to stay well clear of the colonists. Any questions?"

Kalare raised her hand and the Boss acknowledged her.

"Sir—why is it going to be so long before we visit our first colony? We had a Landfall less than three months ago, and we can get back to that planet a lot more quickly since we know where it is and can head straight there."

"Good observation, Kalare. There are three reasons why we won't visit a colony for a while. The first is based on the old adage that the shortest distance between two points is a straight line. Depending on what we discover during the journey, we may find ourselves traveling all the way back to Earth. With that as a potential destination, we're going to chart a heading that gets us there most efficiently and all of our more recent colonies are too far away from that path.

"Second, we must once again traverse the interstellar desert you all may recall that forced us to go years without a Landfall. We'll be able to get through it far faster than the first time since we now have it charted, but even with FTL the distances involved in space travel mean it's sometimes just painfully slow.

"Finally, we want to allow time for the civilians working with us to become more active participants in the operations of the Ship. The odds are high we may encounter hostile aliens as we revisit some of these colonies. We took the planets by force in many cases, so we should expect that other species may have subsequently done the same. We have no reason to do anything but immediately leave any system if we discover a threat, but we must still be prepared to defend ourselves." The Boss gestured toward Rege and the other civilians who sat with him. "These four are now part of the Flight Ops staff, and you should all treat them the same way you would any clueless cadet who was just starting out. They will be working with Flight, Scan, Threat, and Weps."

The Boss pointed at each civilian as he named their new stations and it took all of Zax's control to not outwardly react when he saw that Rege had been assigned as Mini-Threat. He would have to share a station with the insane civilian and train the man! The Boss had to know the history between them—why would he ever make such an assignment?

"That's it—you're dismissed. Expect final confirmation later today, but we should return to our regular duty rotations in Flight Ops starting tomorrow. Get some rest. We're going to be busy."

The compartment exploded in tumultuous discussion as clumps of people considered the details the Boss had shared. A sly grin formed on Rege's lips as he stood and strode across the room toward Zax. Any interactions with the civilian would be intolerable with the shock of having to work so closely with him still fresh. Zax stood and ignored Kalare's calls for him to wait as he bolted from the compartment.

CHAPTER SEVEN

You're right, Alpha.

The Flight Boss returned to his quarters following the meeting with the new Flight Ops team. He was on the verge of apoplexy given how Rege had strolled in late, so the Boss took a circuitous route that allowed him to stretch his legs and clear his head. The walk only served to increase his agitation thanks to the sheer volume of civilians who clogged the passageways. Whereas in the past one might see a random maintenance worker or two in this part of the Ship, the civilians had overrun the area in the week since the Revolution. Almost like vermin. Almost.

When the Boss reached his quarters, he removed his workcap and threw it toward a hook affixed to the bulkhead across the room. It was a well-practiced maneuver, but the hat missed its mark and tumbled to the deck. The Boss ignored it and went instead to his desk. He tossed his chewed-up cigar into the waste bin and his spirits lifted in anticipation of his favorite ritual.

The rich, glorious scent of tobacco wafted out as the Boss opened his humidor and revealed a stack of precious cigars ten wide and five deep. He closed his eyes and took a dozen circular breaths. Whether it was from the breathing or the sight and smell of his cigars, the Boss's pulse dropped ten beats almost instantaneously. He reached for his cutter and, as always, appreciated its heft. It was not some generic piece of crap spat out by a Replicator, but instead had been handcrafted around a blade the Boss lifted off the corpse of an alien he killed many years earlier. The cutter removed the end of the cigar with precision. The Boss put it in his mouth and took a long, unlit draw. Life would be nearly perfect with a fresh new cigar every day, but even he didn't have enough power and influence to support that level of excess.

Power. What did the word even mean any more with the civilians running the show? Yes—the Boss still had authority over the Crew, but Imair was showing a propensity to exert far more control than the figurehead he had initially assumed she'd become. His Plug flashed a notification, and the Boss sighed when he recognized the source of the inbound communication request.

"Hello, Alpha. What do you need?"

"Good morning, Boss. I just became aware of the new duty assignments for Flight Ops and wanted to verify something. You've assigned Rege to be Mini-Threat. This means he will be in close contact with Cadet Zax, and this creates a combustible situation given their recent history together."

Yet again with the second-guessing of his maneuvers around the boy. The Boss was playing a tricky game with the Ship's core Artificial Intelligence, but he had to stick with it if he was to have any chance of success.

"I understand the concern, Alpha. I've given the situation a lot of thought, and this was the approach I believed would best satisfy the long-term goals we've discussed. Is there something specific you would suggest I do differently?"

The AI paused uncharacteristically before responding.

"If you feel the situation is under control, then who am I to question your plans? On a different topic, I was speaking with President Imair and she has a list of requests that I wanted to discuss with you before I took any action."

"Wait—what? You communicated with Imair directly?" The Boss's initial frustration with Alpha was tipping toward rage. *"Did I not tell you that any communications with the civilians should only be done in my presence? Why would you contravene a direct order like that?"*

"Sir—I am not here to serve you alone. I serve the Ship, the Mission, and the command structure in that order. My understanding, provided by you, is that after Order Sixty-Six there was a legitimate transfer of final command authority from the Captain to a new civilian organization with President Imair at its head. If I am given instructions by a human who has appropriate command authority, I must follow those instructions. To do otherwise would violate my programming. I will do whatever I can to best reconcile your instructions with this situation. That is why I came to you before I took action on her requests.

"Furthermore, I am curious, sir, as to why you are so sensitive about this matter. Is there anything in particular you are concerned about President Imair learning through her interactions with me?"

The Boss paused for a deep breath. He absolutely had concerns—loads of them. Particularly around any discussion of Order Sixty-Six. What he was comfortable sharing with Alpha was an entirely different matter. Time to deflect.

"You're correct, Alpha. I was being unreasonable in my expectations and my reaction to you. I haven't slept much since the Revolution, and it has been nothing but nonstop political maneuvering since then. I always find that aspect of my job far more exhausting than anything else, so I'm burnt out."

It was an obvious deflection, so the Boss imagined Alpha wanting to give him a good long stare in an effort to divine the truth. The Boss was no fool, however, and had removed all of the cameras from his compartment when he first moved in decades ago. In theory Alpha only accessed video feeds with explicit permission or a proper order from someone with the appropriate authority, but the Boss took no chances. Rather than allow Alpha to probe deeper on its line of questioning, the Boss changed the subject.

"That reminds me—how are things coming with the scenario evaluations I requested? Have you been able to identify any path by which we might be able to remove the civilians' bomb threat as the source of their power?"

"Most of the permutations I have tested so far yielded nothing but the destruction of the FTL drive and the marooning of the Ship. I'm continuing to explore and expect to have another round of analysis done soon."

The Boss smiled. The AI was a major pain in his ass sometimes, particularly given the angles he was forced to play right now, but there was nothing better in terms of brute horsepower for brainstorming and following each option through to every possible conclusion. There was no obvious way to neutralize the civilian bomb threat, but the Boss would be shocked if Alpha failed to identify at least a couple of viable plans given enough time to crunch the scenarios. He just needed to keep deftly playing both of the conflicts he was managing—against the civilians and against the Ship's AI.

"Thanks, Alpha. Let's get back to the requests that President Imair made."

CHAPTER EIGHT

Sir, you already answered the question.

Zax woke early the next day after a fitful night's sleep. His stomach was like a ball of knots that had been soaked in acid. Logic dictated he shouldn't worry about working alongside Rege. It was impossible for the civilian to harm him with the Revolution over. However, every thought about the greasy sociopath triggered strong emotions centered on death.

The engineering cadet who died so Rege could make a point.

Rege's brother who died so Zax could live.

Nolly.

Kalare.

Of course Kalare hadn't actually died, but Zax's memories from when he chose to sacrifice her life rather than use his blaster to kill Rege provoked the worst of his guilt and anxiety.

When reveille finally sounded, he skipped breakfast in favor of an extra-long shower (twenty demerits). There was no way he would keep food down for long so he soaked for a while instead in an effort to clear his head. The shower didn't cure him, but it did provide enough benefit that he walked to his training session with the cadets from Gamma Cadre with a slight bounce to his step. He arrived early so he sat and focused on positive thoughts while he waited for his students. His last meeting with the group had not been a pleasant one, and Zax was relieved this would be his final class with them since they were about to move on to a new instructor.

There was a markedly different feeling in the air as the Gammas walked in. A week ago there had been nervous energy about the rampant unrest, and Zax had tried to calm the group and provide them with positive perspectives of the civilians. This memory was particularly ironic given the events that took place later that same day. The group now bounded in with enthusiasm. Zax was trying to figure out what might be causing such excitement when a hand went up. It was the cadet who had verbally sparred with him during their last meeting. Zax acknowledged the boy with more than slight trepidation.

"Sir—I've heard all kinds of rumors about what happened at the end of the Revolution and the role you played. Is it true that you killed twenty civilians and saved the Flight Boss's life? That's amazing, but I'm not surprised because I've always been so impressed with you. What can you tell us that we haven't already heard on the newsvid?"

Zax kept his expression neutral while his emotions roiled. The boy had openly mocked Zax the last time they saw each other, and here he was fawning all over him. What was different about Zax? Nothing. The boy's change in attitude was solely due to rumors about what Zax may or may not have done. How shallow. Zax silently stoked his indignation until he was ready to unleash a cutting torrent that would rub the boy's face in his hypocrisy.

Zax opened his mouth but then stopped. What purpose would expressing his anger and revulsion serve? It would provide a hit of self-righteous satisfaction, but it wouldn't change anything. The boy shouldn't be faulted for his attitude. He was only a product of the system that created him—a system that stratified every human on the Ship into levels of relative worth. Zax's rage needed to be with that system, not with this kid who simply manifested it. He paused for a sec and then delivered an entirely different response.

"I'm sorry to disappoint you and the rest of the class, but unfortunately I'm not at liberty to discuss those events. Let me just say that what you've seen on the newsvid is but a small slice of the actual story."

The boy was visibly disappointed, as were the other cadets, but they acted as if they had expected a similar answer. Zax remembered the emotions associated with being that age. Feeling like you had already accomplished everything and should be an equal member of the Crew when in fact you were still just a child with so very much left to learn. Zax set aside the last lesson he was supposed to deliver (one hundred demerits) and instead gifted them with exciting information to use as social currency with their peers.

"I learned yesterday that we're heading back toward Earth. This isn't a surprise given everything we heard during the Revolution, but now it has been confirmed. The Omegas and President Imair will finalize plans soon, and it sounds like we will start traveling that way in a few days. At some point in the next months, we will make our first ever visit to one of our colonies."

Zax captured the full attention of the Gammas and they stared back at him wide-eyed. Time to impart some last measure of academic value while he had them engaged.

"Let's pretend we're heading straight back to Earth rather than stopping at any colonies. Who can tell me how long it will take for us to get there?"

A hand went up from one of the boys who rarely spoke and Zax called on him.

"If we're just retracing our steps, sir, then it will take the same amount of time we've been traveling. Around 5,000 years, sir."

"Wrong. Ten demerits for being incorrect, but I'm going to award you twenty credits for being the first to jump in and for speaking up for the first time in a while. Who can explain to the cadet the reason why he's wrong?"

The girl who always sat up front raised her hand and spoke when Zax nodded at her.

"Respectfully, sir, there isn't only one reason why he's wrong. First, his answer doesn't take into account that we actually know the fastest and most direct route back to Earth from where we are right now thanks to all of the prior scanning data that's in the Ship's records. When we left Earth, we were heading into unknown territory. A great deal of time during the last 5,000 years has been spent wandering around blindly searching for those few planets that sustain life.

"Second, we've spent an awful lot of time over the course of our journey standing still. We've established thousands of colonies, and each of those typically involved hanging around for weeks of scouting missions and preparations. Not to mention all of the times we've found some other intelligent species on an attractive enough planet that we decided to invest the time to evict the aliens.

"Finally, I have to believe that if we want to get to Earth as fast as possible, we can increase our pace of Transits. When we were heading out into the unknown there was no need to rush. This was particularly true once we realized habitable planets were far fewer in number than Earth's scientists believed. Understanding how much longer the Mission would take than planned, captains throughout the years have maintained a Transit pace that is far less than we can tolerate if we want to get somewhere quickly."

Zax beamed at the cadet. It was impossible to explain it any better.

"One hundred credits for not falling into the trap I set when I said '*the* reason' and another five hundred for such a perfect answer. I've run some numbers over the last day and have estimated that, if we head straight back to Earth right now, it will take us approximately twelve years to arrive. This is based on performing one Transit per day which is the upper limit of where we know there are zero negative side effects. That's just a rough estimate based on information I gathered quickly from the public Ship's logs, but it should be correct within a year or two in either direction. What would we find when we got there?"

Zax acknowledged a girl who sat in the middle of the room.

"We'll find a dead planet. Right, sir?"

"Yes. Absolutely. This Ship was only launched after the best minds on Earth realized the planet was doomed. Since all of those folks then left as part of the original Crew, it's absolutely impossible for anyone who remained behind to have stopped that slide into destruction. So, if the other humans out here exploring the universe aren't coming from Earth, where are they coming from?"

Silence. Zax made eye contact with every cadet in the room. Most looked away in an effort to avoid being called on, but even those who held his gaze did so without offering an answer.

"Come on," Zax prodded, "you mean to tell me that none of you have any ideas?"

"Sir, you already answered the question." It was the first boy who had spoken, and his tone was perhaps straying back into mocking territory. "You confirmed what all of us already understood. Earth is dead. That means the only other humans out here came from one of our colonies. Do you really expect anyone to believe that any colonists we've left behind, even the very earliest ones who've had 5,000 years to advance, might engage in interstellar travel?"

"I agree that any of our colonies would be hard pressed to leave their planet even after 5,000 years. Not if they were given 25,000 years, however. After that amount of time, I think it's not only possible, but likely, that at least one colony should reach that point in their advancement."

The room erupted in excited chatter. The girl in the front row raised her voice with a question.

"Sir—my understanding has always been that using the FTL doesn't result in any time dilation. Are you saying that's incorrect?"

Zax smiled. "Glad to see I'm not the only cadet who ever studied something that wasn't covered in the lessons. One hundred credits. There are a lot of blank looks around the room, though. Can you please explain to the others what you mean by *time dilation*?"

"The effect of time dilation was confirmed back when Earth first sent satellites into orbit, sir. Scientists discovered that clocks aboard those satellites moved at slightly different rates than clocks back on the ground. This effect became even more pronounced as humanity traveled further away from Earth. If someone on a spacecraft travels far enough and fast enough, when they return to their origin they will have experienced the passage of less time than what elapsed at home. This effect gets more and more pronounced the closer you travel to the speed of light, but it doesn't happen at all when we Transit faster than light."

"One hundred credits. You're on a roll today." The girl had clearly mastered the concept, but the expressions among the rest of the cadets suggested she might be the only one. Zax pressed on regardless. "You're also absolutely correct when you say that our FTL technology does not result in any time dilation. I'm going to leave the discussion about why that's true for a future instructor, however, as it's far beyond anything this group is prepared to understand today. So if the FTL doesn't cause time dilation, and yet I'm insisting that our earliest colonies have experienced somewhere around 20,000 years' worth of additional time than we have, what are you missing?"

Zax let the silence go on for three mins. He had given up hope of anyone offering an answer when the first boy spoke up again without raising his hand.

"It isn't the FTL which causes the time dilation. It's when we're moving without using the FTL."

"Correct! Fifty credits for getting the answer, though I have to hit you with ten demerits for not having raised your hand and another ten for not calling me *sir*." Zax had chosen the high road earlier and not slammed the boy for his hypocrisy, but he wasn't above exacting a slight bit of revenge for the prior abuse he had suffered. "Can you please explain to the other cadets what you're talking about."

The boy made a face at the mention of demerits. He acted like he wanted to retort but then sat up straight instead. "Well, *sir*, the Ship isn't moving right now because of all the work being done to recover from the Revolution. Most of the time that isn't true."

"Inertial dampeners!"

It was the girl in the front row again. She had slapped her forehead with the heel of her palm when she spoke out. Zax gestured for her to continue.

"My apologies for the interruption, sir. I was disappointed to realize I had been so stupid with my earlier answer. Our inertial dampeners make us feel like the Ship isn't moving even though at full impulse power we're traveling at 99.9 percent the speed of light."

"Well done, cadet. Can you explain to the others what inertial dampeners are?"

"Certainly, sir. The force of inertia creates strict limits on how fast spacecraft can accelerate or decelerate if there are humans on board. That's why our fighter pilots only transfer their consciousness to their craft. Scientists back on Earth spent hundreds of years trying to address the effects of inertia but never succeeded until the Ship. Counterintuitively, it becomes easier to dampen inertia as the mass of the body that is being compensated for increases. That is why they finally succeeded once they had something as massive as our asteroid to work with."

"Great answer. One hundred credits. My favorite thing from that period on Earth was how frequently this technology was referenced in their popular entertainment before it was actually invented. Inertial dampeners were typically a plot device to quiet the more knowledgeable observers who said space travel wasn't possible in the manner in which it was often portrayed." Zax checked the time and then stood up. "I'd love to continue this discussion, but unfortunately I've got to get to Flight Ops for my first shift since it's been rebuilt. I likely won't see you cadets again as an instructor, though I suppose it's possible. Perhaps one of you might be good enough to qualify for the Pilot Academy someday, and I'll be your trainer there."

With those last passive aggressive reminders to the Gammas about how far he had risen since they last saw him, Zax left the compartment. The afterglow of a fun discussion soon faded as the reality of what awaited him in Flight Ops returned.

CHAPTER NINE

Can you hear me?

Zax entered Flight Ops to find a compartment nearly the same as when he had last been there a year ago. And yet, it was completely different. The biggest change was the people. Between those Crew who had moved on to other duty stations since Zax had worked there last and those who were killed when the civilians blew up the compartment last week, they were a group he had mostly never met. The two most important exceptions were Kalare and the Boss, the latter of whom looked up and acknowledged Zax as he stood at the threshold of the compartment.

"Cadet Zax—welcome to the new and improved Flight Ops. It's good to have you back. The Threat chair hasn't been the same without you."

The Omega's tone was genuine, but Zax fought to present a pleasant demeanor back to the man. He drew strength from Kalare, who sat in the Flight chair, and her smile of greeting. He stood tall and looked the Boss straight in the eye.

"It's a pleasure to be back, sir. I can't say enough about how much I appreciate the opportunity to serve here alongside you and the rest of the Flight Ops team again. Thank you for the opportunity. I won't let you down."

He was charging headfirst into danger, but when he accepted the Boss's offer to return a week ago, Zax did so knowing he would have to fully commit. He would be a team of one until he dug up enough evidence to convince Kalare the Boss was indeed behind Mikedo's death and the attempt on both their lives, but he was confident he would eventually win her to his side. In the meantime, he had to sell the Boss that he was dedicated to whatever the Omega wanted him to do. Distasteful, sure, but nowhere near as hard to swallow as a lifetime spent surrounded by sewage.

Zax turned toward the Threat chair and was pleased to discover Rege had not yet arrived. He checked the time, and when he found the shift was about to start, Zax allowed himself to dream that perhaps Rege had been reassigned elsewhere. He sat down and lost himself in the configuration for the newly installed Threat station. Fifteen mins later the compartment hatch opened, but Zax didn't bother to look up until the Boss spoke.

"Civilian—what do you think you're doing strolling in fifteen mins late for your very first shift?"

The tone of the Omega's voice brought everyone's attention to the hatch where Rege stood with a look of pure insolence. The Boss icily held the civilian's gaze until Rege turned and, without a word, walked toward Zax. His mouth twisted into a smirk as he approached.

"Good morning, young Zax. How are—"

"Civilian! What makes you think you can disturb my compartment yet again? Threat—please help your idiotic mini understand proper protocol, and get him configured with a subvoc so I don't have to hear his damn voice again."

Rege directed a baleful gaze toward the Boss, but the Omega had already turned his attention elsewhere. The civilian's face flashed crimson after being publicly mocked and then just as quickly ignored. Zax suppressed a smile. It was going to be rough enough working with Rege given how the man held Zax at least partially responsible for his brother's death, but Zax didn't need to give the civilian a reason to despise him even more. He reached for the subvoc and handed it to Rege as he addressed the civilian with a whisper.

"The rule in here is that you only speak aloud when you're sharing information that is needed by everyone in the compartment. If you're having a private conversation with anyone, it should be done silently. Crew who are old enough use their Plugs for direct communication. Younger cadets—and I suppose anyone else who hasn't been Plugged In—use subvocs."

Rege took the device from Zax and gaped at it as if it was some kind of alien artifact. "What the hell am I supposed to do with this?"

Zax lost his composure and laughed out loud at the civilian's ineptitude. Rege's response was an immediate and intense look of hatred that made Zax fear the long-term repercussions.

"I'm sorry. I'm not trying to make you feel bad or anything. It's just entirely foreign to me that you don't know how to use a subvoc. Crew children use these in the creche before we even learn how to walk. You need to slip it around your throat, and then it will take care of the rest."

Rege stared dubiously at the device which wasn't big enough to fit around his wrist much less get over his head and down around his throat. Did the attendants in the creche ever get frustrated with trying to teach kids such basic life skills? At least toddlers have an excuse—they're toddlers. Perhaps that was the secret for training Rege successfully—Zax needed to treat him like a child.

"Give it a slight tug as if you're trying to stretch it larger, and it will open to fit over your head. Once it's around your throat, it will automatically close and position itself."

Rege almost dropped the subvoc when he startled as it opened in response to him following Zax's instructions. The civilian placed the device around his throat and stared at Zax with wide-eyed apprehension as it constricted and positioned the various components at the appropriate spots on his face.

"Can you hear me?"

"What the—whoa!"

Zax glanced over at the Flight Boss who was engrossed in something on a screen and didn't react to Rege's verbal exclamation. He needed to get the civilian to remain quiet before that changed.

"The Boss isn't going to care one bit about your relationship with Imair if you don't shut up while you're working in here. I don't know what punishment he might give you since you're not on the Leaderboard, but I can promise you don't want to find out. Nod your head if you hear and understand me."

Rege nodded and his earlier expression of surprise was replaced with one that was once again closer to malice.

"Boy—if you think you're going to keep talking down to me like this, you're going to find out what punishment I might give you."

Zax went wide-eyed in response to the threat and Rege responded similarly.

"Wait—did you just hear that? I didn't say anything at all. I was thinking it to myself. It's true, but I was going to save it for later."

Zax suppressed the grin that was poised on his lips. He needed to treat Rege not only like a toddler but more specifically like a toddler who was on the verge of a dangerous tantrum.

"There's a thin line between thought and intention to speak. It's great that you learned the lesson so quickly with the low stakes of speaking with me privately rather than the Boss or all of Flight Ops. You'll probably have another couple of accidental outbursts during today's shift, but I've always heard that Crew toddlers get the hang of this in only a couple of hours. You're probably at least as smart as a Crew toddler, right?"

"Be careful, boy. And I'm saying this to you on purpose in case it isn't obvious on my face. I'm still under Imair's orders from the Revolution to not kill you, but I can't be responsible for any accidents that might happen when you walk past a malfunctioning airlock."

Zax ignored the threat and focused on the first part of what Rege said. Imair had protected Zax during the Revolution? His head swam, and the surprise must have registered on Zax's face because Rege's expression transformed from menace to perverse delight.

"You didn't know? What did you think, Zax, that you somehow tricked me into not killing you all on your own? Without her protection, you would have been dead as soon as I had my brother's knife back to carve you up with."

Imair had made it clear she had not intended to kill Nolly, but her lack of significant remorse had left Zax feeling she was not that much better than Rege. Why was she shielding Zax—especially after he had tried to disrupt her plans?

"Cadet Zax," the Boss's voice interrupted Zax's confusion, "You got that civilian using a subvoc without him somehow hurting himself. Those must be pretty impressive training skills. Now let's see you do the impossible and make him the least bit useful."

Rege swiveled toward the Boss. This time the Omega locked eyes with the civilian and held his gaze for a min. The civilian's body tensed and he clenched his fists until the Boss delivered a dismissive smirk and turned away. Zax took advantage of the man's rage being focused elsewhere to get redirected toward work. He pointed at the Threat board.

"What do you know about any of this stuff?"

"I think you already know the answer to that question, boy. Why don't we agree that you can speak to me like a child one last time to explain it all?"

Teach a civilian with a hair-trigger temper everything about working the Threat board in the span of a quick conversation. While he was still learning how to communicate over subvoc. It was a lose-lose proposition, but what choice did Zax have?

"Sure. Let me give you six months' worth of training in five mins. No problem. Our job on the Threat board is to monitor for any signs of danger to the Ship and call out anything we see, so the Boss and other folks around us can evaluate and choose the appropriate action. Generally, a threat takes the form of aliens in the midst of battle, but sometimes it may be as simple as an errant space rock.

"I'm in charge of the board, and whenever someone calls out to Threat, they want something from me. You are Mini-Threat and your workstation is functionally identical to mine so you can watch everything I do and soak in as much as you can. Each functional area is arranged the same way with a primary and a mini. Just because I'm the one in charge doesn't mean you can sit back and relax because the Boss is well-known for calling out to the various minis to be sure they're paying attention. If he asks you a question, give him the answer. If you don't know the answer, admit you don't know instead of trying to fake it. Outside of that, you should not speak aloud or communicate with anyone other than me. Understood?"

The civilian nodded with the faintest hint of a smile creasing his mouth.

"Thank you, cadet. When do we start doing this for real?"

"You're Imair's right hand—shouldn't you know when the action is going to start?"

Rege grinned before he replied and it made Zax's blood go cold.

"Soon. All of the action will definitely start soon."

CHAPTER TEN

One last thing.

Imair was running late, but one benefit of being in charge was the certainty that meetings wouldn't start without her. Especially a meeting to make the final decision about their journey. The amount of critical work since the Revolution was never-ending, and Imair was excited to finally bring the senior leadership together again to reach agreement on plans for heading back toward Earth. As she approached the compartment, she found the Boss about to enter ahead of her.

"Good morning, Boss. I guess I'm not the only one running late today."

The man stopped and turned around. "My apologies, Madam President. It's good I won't be disrupting a meeting that has already started. I still haven't gotten used to walking everywhere. I'm looking forward to getting the Tube up and running again."

"Not a problem at all. In fact, I'm glad we ran into each other this way. I haven't seen you in more than a week. I was starting to worry that perhaps you've been choosing to avoid me."

The Boss's cheek muscles clenched as he gnawed his cigar. Imair suppressed a grin about the man unconsciously revealing his stress yet again.

"The only thing I've been avoiding, ma'am, is sleep. And that isn't by choice. I'm never comfortable when the Ship is sitting around for more than a couple of days. I know we've had a lot of repairs to make so I absolutely understand why, but I still feel stir crazy. I've convinced myself that if I work a few extra hours a day, it will make all the difference in us moving again."

"I admire your work ethic, Boss. All the same, once we begin our new journey, I'd like to be certain we don't go that long without checking in with each other. Let's plan on meeting one-on-one at least every few days. The more opportunities we have to get comfortable with each other, the more effective this relationship is going to be."

"By all means, ma'am."

The Boss moved to enter the compartment as if he was trying to escape from Imair as quickly as possible. What better time to catch the man off guard?

"One last thing. I've gone back and reviewed the video from the brig. There was something the Captain said near the end that's been bothering me. She was pretty agitated at the notion the Ship's AI instigated her removal. I've tried to get more details about the Order Sixty-Six protocol and its history directly from Alpha, but every time I broach the subject the AI deflects it. Can you help me understand?"

The Boss paused before turning back to Imair. His outward appearance was 99 percent calm and composed, but his face bore the barest hint of agitation.

"I don't know how much more there is to understand, ma'am, beyond what happened on the vid. The Captain knew what was coming. When people are about to die, they'll do whatever they can to prolong the inevitable. She picked that topic thinking it would keep me talking. She was wrong. We can chat further about it during those one-on-one meetings you suggested, but shouldn't we get into this meeting? You've got a lot of busy people sitting around in there waiting for us."

Yet another deflection around the topic. Imair was certain there was something odd at play, but the Boss was clearly not going to give it up easily. She nodded and gestured for the man to proceed inside. She followed and the compartment went silent as she entered.

Once again the room was overcrowded, but this time the group had arranged themselves with a fair bit of integration. More than one team, Crew and civilians alike, were mixed together. Rege remained the oddball as he stood off to the side with no one else nearby. The hollowness of his cheeks was starting to fill out, and he was even developing the slightest paunch. It was amazing what a few weeks of high quality food accomplished after a lifetime of deprivation.

"Sorry I'm late, everyone. The Boss just chided me, ever so politely, about how busy all of you are, so let's jump right in. First, give me an update on all of the repairs and modifications to the Ship."

A civilian stood and listed a dozen compartments that had been rebuilt following extensive bomb damage during the Revolution.

"OK. What about the modifications we wanted to make? For example, the worker safety improvements in the sewage treatment cavern?"

"I'm sorry, ma'am." The civilian speaking was clearly uncomfortable and shuffled back and forth on her feet. "We haven't been able to tackle any of those yet. We're working as fast as we can, but you said we needed to get ready for travel again ASAP. We've put all of our resources into the work that's most critical. We'll redirect the teams to those improvements as they have time, but we've still got weeks of effort just to fix the remaining workspaces that are more important."

"What about resource leveling and redistribution? How are those efforts going?"

Once again the civilian gave the impression she wanted to be anywhere else in the universe rather than giving her update. "Similar story, ma'am. The good news is that we've arranged for all critical civilians to have access to Crew mess halls, so all of our most important staff are getting the food they need. The bad news is that we can't just fling the doors open to everyone else because it would be chaos. We've got teams identified who will evaluate different solutions and eventually make sure all ten million civilians get access to better food, but we need more time for the task to reach the top of their priority list."

Imair's increasing frustration approached the boiling point. Even more so when she witnessed the trace of a self-satisfied smile on the Boss. He had once railed at her about the need to make difficult choices as a leader, and here she was confounded by those same choices. She had to do better by the ten million civilians. She had to give them a better life. It started with locating the other space-faring humans, though, and solving how to get everyone off this Ship and into a sustainable future. With that as the goal, a few more weeks of the status quo wasn't going to make a difference. They were making tough choices, but they were the right choices. Her agitation waned as she sighed and then spoke.

"I'm not happy, but I understand. It took millennia for the Ship's society to get into the state which led to the Revolution, so we shouldn't be upset if undoing that damage takes a little longer than hoped. Thank you for the update. I'll look forward to putting all of this behind us given a few more weeks' effort." Imair turned to the Boss. "Flight Boss—can you please give us an update on the planning and preparations for the journey back toward Earth."

The Boss stood. "Ma'am—we've studied the Scan records and identified the best paths that meet the goals you've laid out. We understand you want to head toward Earth on a routing that lets us visit as many of our colonies as possible. With over 20,000 colonies spread far and wide in our wake, we've assumed you intend to visit a small percentage of them. We've generated two possible courses. The first will have us visit recent colonies within weeks and puts us within easy reach of a larger number of colonies overall. Choosing this path takes us off the optimal line back to Earth and therefore incurs an additional five years of travel if that becomes our final destination.

"The second option not only postpones contact with any former colonies for six months but also puts us within easy reach of fewer overall. This routing is far more efficient about delivering us to Earth, though, and gets us there in a little more than twelve years."

"Thank you, Boss. How does this process work? What happens next?"

"The choice is yours, Madam President. You decide which path you want to take and give us the order. We'll announce the first Transit and be under way before the end of the day."

Imair deliberated. She wanted to visit their colonies sooner than six months, but a longer delay before any action might actually be in their best interests. It would provide sufficient breathing room for all of the teams to complete the work needed to fix the Ship's broken society. If that same routing also returned them to Earth that much faster, then all the better. There really was no choice to make.

"Thank you, Boss. I want us to make best possible speed homeward. Let's get some stories on the newsvid that provide everyone with an overview of the plan and explain why we won't make Landfall for six months. Most people will probably be disappointed by that delay like I am, but we can help them understand why it's for the best. Let's get started!"

CHAPTER ELEVEN

Take it or leave it.

The three small steps had appeared to Adan nearly as insurmountable as Everest, so he wasn't surprised when he lost his footing between the second and third. Markev was in far better condition and steadied him before he toppled to the ground. Thankfully, this private entrance to the Chancery was hidden from the press, and there wouldn't be any prying lenses to capture Adan's moment of weakness. He had no business traveling within twenty-four hours of returning to Earth after such a long time spent in zero-g, but the Chancellor's aides had made it clear their invitation was really a non-negotiable summons.

Markev checked his firearm at the door and, once they passed an unobtrusive security screening, they were escorted back to an anteroom. As famous as

Adan had already been, it was generally in name only. Very few people recognized him in public. It was obvious that situation had changed as the head of every staffer whipped around with some mixture of shock and awe as he walked through the crowded hallways. Apparently, once you've shocked the world's governments by navigating a few billion tons of space rock into low-Earth orbit, the news media will feature your face nonstop. On the bright side, recruiting for the mission wouldn't need nearly as big a marketing budget given all the free news coverage.

    The door opened and a young male aide stepped out and signaled for them to enter. Adan had briefly met the Chancellor at an event years earlier but had never visited the Chancery. The building with its white facade was hundreds of years old, and in that time many world-altering orders had emanated from the relatively small, oval office where the most powerful leaders in humanity had long resided. For the past fifty years, the office's occupant had held dominion over 10 percent of the Earth's citizens collectively known as the West, and the current Chancellor had ruled for nearly half of that period. The woman sitting behind the desk had an outward appearance which reflected her advanced age, though almost all who dealt with her agreed that her mental capacity and overall tenacity was that of someone two-thirds younger. She was not to be trifled with. Adan approached and extended his hand in greeting.

"Good morning, Madam Chancellor. I appreciate the invitation to visit the Chancery as I've only ever seen it on the news. How may I be of service?"

"Cut the crap, Adan. You know full well why you're here."

The strident voice behind Adan belonged to the Chancellor's Chief of Staff. Jania had recently inherited the position from her father, and all of the resultant press coverage suggested the daughter was even more intense than he had been. She glared at Adan for a good long moment to make sure he understood who was really in charge in this room, and then she gestured for him to sit on the sofa opposite her. Markev took up a standing position behind his boss. The Chancellor walked over and sat next to Jania. She leaned forward with her hands clasped and her elbows across the thighs of her navy-blue pantsuit. She couldn't have presented more like a sweet grandmother if she tried, though Adan recognized a visage far different when he focused on her eyes while she spoke.

"Thanks for coming, Adan. I know it was a lot to ask given that you've just returned from such a long journey. You have to understand, though, that you've created quite the situation for us here. You raised holy hell when sensors detected that asteroid coming toward us and we hadn't yet received your transmission explaining it was under your control. Going radio silent rather than responding to our requests for more information only served to make things worse. I had all kinds of military and security advisors crawling up my ass demanding that we make an example of you on the grounds of national security risk. I think the most commonly used expression suggested throwing you into a deep, dark hole somewhere."

The Chancellor smiled throughout her introduction. Jania, on the other hand, exuded more and more agitation. Adan mentally chalked the young advisor up as a likely leader of the 'deep dark hole' faction as the older woman continued to speak.

"So today, we're going to explore in great detail exactly why it is that you've done what you've done and what you plan to do next. I don't want any games. Give us the complete truth about what you're planning, and then we'll figure out what we're going to do about it. If I sense any prevarication, then I'm going to be forced to listen to some of the dissenting opinions among my advisors about how we handle you. Do we understand each other?"

Adan was being given a valuable lesson in the difference between power and influence. His wealth and prestige allowed him to strongly influence the thoughts and actions of almost everyone he came into contact with. These two women had the power to make him disappear. Forever. Big difference. He took a deep breath and dove in.

"My pleasure, Madam Chancellor. We all know that Earth's climate has passed a tipping point from which it will absolutely not recover. With all due respect, what exactly are you doing about it? What is humanity doing about it? The East has established successful outposts in the belt and the outer ring, but those will never become more than small islands of life. Yes—they're also terraforming Mars, but I've studied the data at length and it's abundantly clear that meaningful results are 10,000 years away. Meanwhile, it's obvious to anyone with a pulse that this planet's ability to sustain our species is certainly measured in tens of years rather than thousands.

"I'm building an ark. My new asteroid will serve as its bedrock and all of its titanium ore will be the material for towers that ascend kilometers high. This lifeboat cannot rescue all of humanity, but it will save enough of the best to ensure the long-term survival of our species. Never again will humankind place all of its bets on one single home world. We will spend the next hundred years scattering ourselves across the universe. Some of these new colonies will die off, but most will thrive. Together they will ensure that humanity's shining light does not get extinguished but instead illuminates every corner of the universe for the next million years."

Adan sat back and waited. The Chancellor continued to stare at him while Jania glared out the window. The two women finally made eye contact and the younger one nodded. The Chancellor turned back to Adan.

"I had thought this was somehow just another of your money-making schemes. Jania tried to convince me you had a bigger vision, but frankly the one time we met you struck me as disinterested in the rest of the human race. Here you are spending all of this time and money trying to actually save it. You surprise me, sir. What can we do to help?"

"Well, Madam Chancellor, there are two ways in which you can be of service. The first is you can stay the hell out of my way. Nothing against you personally, but every time I've seen your bureaucrats get involved in something it takes forever and ends poorly. I want this to move incredibly fast and the only way that can happen is if it moves my way. You can try to tie me up with regulations and lawsuits, but then I'll just pull the rock out of orbit and do this elsewhere. Maybe the East would be interested in having me do the work with their people out in Mars orbit instead."

The Chancellor raised an eyebrow at Adan's mention of the East. He was jumping into a dangerous game making demands and threats, but he had to establish early on that he was playing for keeps and was not going to be pushed around. His views were well publicized enough they all knew he would never actually use the East as leverage, but he had to make everyone aware the option was available to him nonetheless.

"I understand my second request is trickier, but it's critical and non-negotiable. Are you familiar with Sirius B, Madam Chancellor?"

The Chancellor shook her head and her reaction came across as entirely genuine. Jania, on the other hand, betrayed some knowledge with a nearly imperceptible widening of her eyes. Adan explained.

"Forty-five years ago your predecessor approved the launch of a small space probe to Sirius B. The mission was intended to validate a secret new propulsion system. That engine was never able to scale up any larger than drone size which is why it has never been put to further use, but the original probe averaged one half the speed of light over the course of its journey. Five years ago it returned.

"Sirius B is the closest white dwarf star to Earth. The purpose of the probe was to return with a sample of the degenerate gas it emits. Our scientists have long believed that degenerate gas would make a tremendous weapon. They are right, and if they had enough time they would crack the puzzle and develop just such a weapon. They don't have enough time, and I have a much better use for that matter. I need you to give all of it to me as fuel for the faster-than-light engine that I have developed. I spent our trip to the belt finalizing the design, and as soon I can secure the gas I will be ready to test it out."

Jania had gotten progressively more agitated as Adan spoke. She leaned in further and further and her knuckles became whiter and whiter. The Chancellor, on the other hand, leaned back until she was fully reclined against the cushions with a bemused expression on her face.

"Well, sir, you know more about what our government is up to than even I do. I've never heard of this program, but based on Jania's reaction it clearly exists."

"Ma'am—"

"Shut-up, Jania. I don't care. I'm sure this is but one of a thousand black programs that I don't need to know about, so you haven't shared them. I'm immediately clearing Adan and his bodyguard into whatever security level is required to discuss this matter. Do you understand?"

Jania nodded. "Yes, ma'am."

"OK. With that out of the way, do you mind sharing what you know about this program?"

"Not much more than what Adan has already described, ma'am. This is among the top five most highly protected secrets in the history of mankind, so I'm at a complete loss as to how he knows what he does. Regardless—he's got it all correct. The only thing I can add is that our scientists don't share Adan's confidence they will ever crack the code and weaponize the gas. They've concluded it's a dead end and will probably be thrilled to be removed from this operation and let someone else deal with maintaining the gas storage."

The Chancellor smiled. "Well, I can think of two or three others that might round out your top five secret programs, and when our guests have left we should take a few minutes to be sure I understand the complete list. If any of them might be relevant for Adan's project, then we're going to need to get him cleared into those as well."

Adan's ears perked up at the Chancellor's last words. She noticed and smiled at him.

"Yes, Adan, you heard me correctly. You will have our complete cooperation as far as it relates to these two requests. I imagine this will extend to all related requests going forwards, but for obvious reasons I can't make a blanket promise. I will give you my direct line, and if you ever need anything don't hesitate to contact me."

"I'm flattered, Madam Chancellor. I had thought this would require months of painful discussion and mind-numbing negotiation to get to this point. I can't believe you're letting me have this."

"Son—I'm not letting you *have* anything. I am trading what you need for what I need—you just haven't heard the terms yet. My needs are simple. Five hundred thousand slots on the spaceship. I've already had my experts run the numbers in case Jania had guessed right about your plans, and they've told me you were likely building something to transport and sustain somewhere around one million people. Those slots are going to be the most valuable commodity in human history. I realize asking for half is a lot, but that's my offer. Take it or leave it."

Adan kept his smile to himself. The Chancellor's experts had done a fair job of estimating his initial capacity. What they clearly hadn't explained to her was how their calculations anticipated needing the majority of the ship's volume for agriculture production and fuel storage. Relying on conventional space engines for their journey, sufficient food supplies for one million inhabitants would have been tough to squeeze into something even as big as the asteroid. Assuming the FTL engine worked as expected, however, the ability to travel so much further so much faster would drastically decrease the amount of provisions required at the onset. The ship's capacity had increased tenfold under the new assumptions, and that was before considering how many additional colonists Adan intended to bring along in a fashion more like cargo. That was a discussion best left for another day and not anything the Chancellor needed to know right now lest she increase her demands further.

"Five hundred thousand slots is a shockingly fair exchange, ma'am. I only request that we get this in writing for both of our protection."

The Chancellor laughed. "Adan—you're protected by the fact that I continue to smile about you right now rather than frown. If you think a piece of paper is going to make that much of a difference, then fine. Jania will draw it up, and we can sign before you leave. In the meantime, I'll ask you to wait back in the anteroom as I have other guests who are arriving in a moment. It's been a pleasure doing business with you, sir. I will look forward to regular status reports on your progress and a better understanding of the expected timeline, so I can plan for our departure and distribute my invitations accordingly. Good day."

CHAPTER TWELVE

To get us ready for the real thing.

Zax choked down the nutripellet. After suffering them two meals a day for three straight months, he wasn't even upset any longer. He had spent far too much time wallowing in denial (messy, messy) but then passed quickly through rage and depression before finally reaching a state of acceptance. The medics were never going to fix whatever caused him to vomit after FTL Transits. He had to adapt his life accordingly.

Adaptation was even more necessary given the sheer volume of FTL Transits the Ship was engaging in as it sped back toward its colonies. In the past, a typical FTL tempo was one Transit per week. Since resuming travel after the Revolution, the Ship had jumped every single day. At least the powers that be scheduled each Transit to occur right before lunch. After some trial and error, Zax discovered the effects of his problem were minimized if he started and ended his day with nutripellets and ate regular food only at lunchtime. Eating nutripellets twice a day for twelve straight years was unimaginable, though, so he hoped they would stumble upon the mysterious humans sooner than later.

"Zax—are you sure you enjoy coming to breakfast with me every day? You're usually pretty glum, and I wonder if you might be better off not watching me eat."

It was a line of questioning that Kalare pursued at least weekly. Zax appreciated her concern, but he reacted as he always did.

"Thanks for checking, but I still feel the same way. The only thing more depressing than eating so many nutripellets would be eating them off by myself somewhere. Let's not talk about food, please. I can't believe you're finally going to be the trainer for my class this morning. What's your lesson about?"

"I'm teaching today? I better figure something out to talk about then!"

Zax hung his head in disbelief. Kalare waited for a few extra beats and then broke out one of her shrill, braying laughs.

"I'm kidding! I know I'm teaching. But it's true I haven't figured out my whole lesson just yet. I've been too busy thinking about my first actual flight."

Zax smiled. "Are you excited about it?"

Kalare's face lit up. "Yes! I can't believe it's finally here. I understand why we spend so long in the simulators, but the past few months have reached the point where it's entirely boring and repetitive. What about you? Today is your first flight in an Academy simulator. You've got to be pretty fired up about that. Right?"

Zax sighed. "Truthfully, it just feels like more of the same old thing. It will be fun to get into an Academy simulator, sure, but even that will get boring pretty quickly given how much time I've spent in mine. I can't believe I've still got another full year before I fly an actual spacecraft."

"Well, Mr. Smarty-pants, if you already know all of this stuff, why aren't you at the top of your Academy class?"

Kalare was just being her goofy self, but her comment scorched a nerve for Zax. Even though he had promised himself he wouldn't care about beating Mase, having the young cadet constantly perched above him in the Pilot Academy standings rankled. Zax tried to remember that Major Eryn was no doubt doing everything possible to help Mase succeed, and such a leg up was likely the cause of the boy's lead. Regardless, Zax wanted to figure out how to leapfrog to the top spot. One good zinger deserved another, so he launched his own salvo at Kalare.

"I didn't know you knew how to find the Academy standings, much less ever bothered to look at them."

Kalare beamed. "Ha, ha. It's funny because it's true! I have to get going to check on something before I teach your group. We both have big days ahead. What do you say we connect again for dinner?"

"Sounds great. See you then."

Zax balled up his wrappers and threw them toward a waste bin as he made his way to the exit. They bounced back up out of the bin, and Zax approached to pick them up and throw them away. When he did, he discovered the bin was full almost to the brim with apples that appeared fine other than a couple of tiny dark spots here and there. The typical piles of flawless fruit were at the entrance of the mess hall as always, so this was clearly the work of someone who wanted to get rid of anything with the smallest blemish. He had expected that food waste like this would have stopped long ago, but clearly the civilians still hadn't quite gotten around to fixing all of the grievances that triggered their Revolution.

The training room was half-full when Zax arrived. Rather than take his usual seat up front, he grabbed one at the back of the room so that he wouldn't risk being a distraction for Kalare as she led the lesson. A min before the session was supposed to begin, Major Eryn strode into the room. She looked around for a moment and then sat down in the empty seat next to Mase—the one Zax would have otherwise been in. He palmed his forehead at the realization that in trying to help Kalare, he had instead created a situation where the major would be right in front of her.

Kalare walked in with only a few secs to spare. She gave a quick glance toward Major Eryn and then stood at the podium.

"Good morning, class. My name is Kalare and I'm one year ahead of you. I'm here today to help you prepare for your first flight in an Academy simulator. Who can tell me the purpose of using the simulators?"

Without raising his hand or looking up, Mase spoke. "To get us ready for the real thing."

Kalare smiled. "Twenty demerits for being wrong and another twenty for not raising your hand. Does anyone know the right answer?"

Mase didn't react in any fashion to Kalare's assessment of demerits. He had such a massive lead on everyone else in his cadre the number was not a big deal, but Zax still would have expected at least some minor reaction to getting whacked with forty. The boy just sat there with his perpetually fuzzy scalp tilted toward the deck as if he might be nodding off.

Major Eryn, on the other hand, was visibly displeased. Her shoulders tensed and she cocked her head to fix Kalare with a pointed stare. Kalare seemed oblivious as she scanned the room looking for raised hands. There were none, and Zax was about to raise his when Mase spoke again.

"To get us ready for the real thing."

Someone gasped. Kalare kept her expression neutral, but Zax could tell she was perplexed by the boy's outright disrespect. He didn't know if she was aware that Mase was being mentored by Major Eryn, but even if she was Zax suspected the knowledge wouldn't stop her from doing what was right in the situation.

"One hundred demerits for intentionally being wrong again and another one hundred for once more not raising your hand. Do you want to try for five hundred and five hundred, or should we let someone else attempt the answer?"

Zax raised his hand to help Kalare finally move on. She smiled and pointed at him.

"There are three primary reasons. First, it's important to weed out those folks who really have no business flying even though they somehow managed to get into the Academy. Second, we need to make our stupid mistakes now before we ever put an actual fighter at risk. Finally, we need practice with a far greater variety of scenarios than could ever be done in real life."

"Perfect answer! One hundred credits."

Zax wasn't anywhere close to being as excited by the credits as he was by the smile from Kalare that came with them. His delight was short-lived, however, as movement in his peripheral vision caught his eye. It was Major Eryn turning around in her seat. She fixed him with a look that suggested a deep dissatisfaction. Zax turned away and tried to push any concern out of mind as Kalare continued her lesson, but the major's resentful expression was burned front and center in his memory.

CHAPTER THIRTEEN

Today you will fly.

A fter a delicious lunch of solid food enjoyed sitting by himself, Zax headed to the simulator room for his first official flight at the Academy. He took a seat in the front row next to Mase. The boy glanced over as Zax approached but just as quickly turned away without any acknowledgement. They had partnered for the first month and sat next to each other for most of another two, but still the young cadet had not ever said anything to Zax which wasn't absolutely required.

"I knew the answer."

Zax was so shocked to hear any words coming from next to him that he froze. Eventually Mase continued.

"I knew the answer. Your friend bugs me. I've listened to you two laughing in the mess hall all the time. She bugs me. I just wanted to tweak her a bit. Especially with the major watching."

Zax was racking his brain for some reasonable response to the boy when he was surprised a second time in as many mins. Major Eryn entered the room and approached the podium. It was a momentous day for the class so her participation was warranted, but she had largely been in the background for most of their training to date. She cleared her throat and spoke.

"Good morning, cadets. We dispatched another two of your classmates yesterday evening, so that means that ninety-four of you remain to begin this next phase of your training. Today you will fly. In a simulator. The past three months have provided the theoretical grounding necessary for you to survive as a pilot. Now we will see who can translate those concepts out of the classroom and into the simulator. Exactly a year from now, seventy of you will graduate from the simulator to pilot your own spacecraft.

"We have a surprisingly tight race at the top of the Academy standings with Cadet Mase and Cadet Zax locked in a battle for first place. I expect one of them will pull out ahead during the next few months as the flight simulation gets more intense."

The major stared at Mase as she spoke, and Zax fought to keep his face neutral. Of course she expected her pet cadet to pull out ahead. The concern he had to weigh was how much she was willing to artificially influence the outcome if Zax beat Mase on the merits. He refocused on her words.

"In addition to the Academy standings which you are already well-familiar with, today marks the stage in your pilot training when we introduce an additional scoring metric. Your Flight standing will be scored entirely on your performance in the cockpit and tracked separately from the Academy standings. Whichever cadet is at the top of the Flight standings will use the call sign Maverick during your training exercises. Whoever holds this esteemed call sign when you graduate the Academy will be rewarded with their first choices for Flight posting as well as Weapons System Operator."

The major captured Zax's undivided attention with her last sentence. He had briefly considered allowing Mase to beat him in the Flight standings so as to not risk any blowback from Major Eryn, but the discovery he was competing to control his destiny pushed that thought aside. Zax was determined to guarantee his picks for post and WSO. He and Kalare would make an awesome team in a fighter, and Zax was not going to let anything get in the way of that outcome.

"Cadets—please reach below your chair for the helmet you will find there. Place it over your head and it will configure itself."

Zax grabbed his helmet and was shocked to discover it trailed a wire that led back under his seat. Most of the Ship's technology ran wirelessly and it was almost unheard of for anything to connect via an actual hardline. Zax raised his hand and was acknowledge by the major.

"Ma'am—why do the helmets require a wired connection rather than using wireless like everything else on the Ship?"

"Great question, cadet. You probably don't realize this, but our wireless connections are constantly fluctuating in signal strength and sometimes will even cut out for millisecs at a time. This is perfectly normal and well within their acceptable operational profile. Similar to the way pilot chairs require hardlines to ensure a flawless transfer of consciousnesses into and out of our fighters, simulators require wired connections to ensure the highest fidelity transfer of data into and out of your mind. Any glitches caused by normal wireless performance would drastically impact the degree to which our simulators can be used to perfectly evaluate your performance."

Zax nodded and then placed the helmet over his head. He was instantly transported into a virtual fighter. The effect was so lifelike as to induce disorientation that would have been debilitating were it not for the past year's work with his own simulator. Instead, he found that every piece of information and each system control was located exactly where he had grown accustomed to them being. The major's voice cut in over the headset.

"OK, cadets. It's your first day, so you're all on equal footing in terms of being clueless about how everything works. The rules are simple—hunt down and destroy your classmates. The last fighter standing will be named the first Maverick for your class. Engage!"

The threat board in Zax's fighter burst to life as a jumble of simulated craft shot off in all directions. Most appeared to be barely under control as the cadets at their helms tried to figure out what they were doing. Except for one. Mase was on a direct course for him, and the boy's fighter moved like it was being flown by an expert pilot. The young Zeta deftly avoided a few random shots from other classmates and never wavered from his course toward Zax as he was clearly intent on knocking out his closest competition.

Zax throttled his craft in a random and ineffective fashion to give the appearance he was having difficulty getting it under control. He also kept it pointed away from Mase's approach so as to appear as unthreatening as possible. The young boy's fighter continued to close the distance and Zax fired a shot in the opposite direction off into empty space to reinforce his ruse.

Closer.

Closer.

Closer.

At the last possible moment before Mase would be within optimal range to fire, Zax pounded the throttle and his craft executed a perfect 180-degree flip. A plasma bolt seared the space he had occupied a split-sec earlier, and Zax pulled his own trigger as his fighter settled into the proper orientation. An explosion filled his viewscreen and the name Mase disappeared from the threat board.

Zax whooped in appreciation but then turned his focus back to the board. A quick glance revealed that no one else possessed anywhere near the piloting skills of the cadet he had just dispatched. He didn't want to take for granted that others may be laying the same trap he had used to ensnare Mase, so Zax treated each target as if the best pilot on the Ship was at the controls.

Shoot. Kill.

Shoot. Miss. Shoot. Kill.

Shoot, shoot, shoot. Kill. Kill. Kill.

A few mins later, Zax's threat board was devoid of fighters. Only his name remained at the center of the screen until it too faded away and was replaced by the call sign *Maverick*. He did it! Now all he had to do was keep it up for another twenty-one months.

CHAPTER FOURTEEN

Maverick is go for launch.

Kalare approached the high-security hatch. She had walked past it a thousand times during her first fifteen months in the Academy, but she was finally authorized to enter and it opened as she approached. The absolute quiet struck her first. She was the last to arrive, exactly on time, and her sixty-nine remaining classmates stood in silent awe of their new pilot chairs. They had each spent countless hours getting measured, poked, and prodded over the past month to be fitted for these chairs. Each was highly customized for the intended occupant in order to create a perfect bond between human and machine. Major Eryn's voice broke the spell.

"Good morning, cadets. I know many of you worried this day would never come, and for thirty of your classmates it never did. After thousands of hours in the simulator, this is finally the day. Today you will fly. In space. You have nearly reached what, for most of you, will be the absolute pinnacle of your career. We have spent the past month building the chairs you see in front of you. Your chair will be yours as long as you remain in this Academy, and if you graduate it will serve you as long as you remain alive. If you are ever killed in action, your chair will become your coffin when we honor your service and bury you in it. You will float in its embrace for eternity."

Kalare's heart quickened. She took repeated deep breaths in an effort to calm herself. The major continued.

"Today's exercise is simple. All of you can do this with your eyes closed or you would already be gone. You'll be flying solo. No WSOs since this is just a flight test with no weapons. Load up. Launch. Each squadron form up at your rally point, and then perform the maneuvers your instructors described yesterday while maintaining attack formation. Finally, return to the Ship. Are you ready?"

Seventy cadets unleashed full-throated roars. "Ma'am, yes, ma'am!"

Eryn smiled. "Good. Maverick—you have the honor of going first."

At the major's signal Kalare turned toward her chair. Most of her classmates were shocked that Kalare had held the Maverick call sign for almost the entirety of the year it was awarded. She often cared little about what happened in the classroom, so her Academy standings would fluctuate wildly depending on how interested she was in any given day's topic. Operating a fighter, though, was her natural habitat. Almost since the moment she slipped into the cockpit of that mecha during training with Zax, Kalare knew her future lay at the controls of a war machine. Flying the simulator during her Academy training was amazing, but this would finally be the real deal. There was only one problem.

Kalare couldn't breathe.

A technician stood next to her chair and gestured for Kalare to approach, but her feet were stuck to the deck and her mind flooded by a jumble of memories. Two girls floating in space outside a panorama. A beautiful young face frozen for eternity in a terrified scream. Warm urine washing over her legs.

Kalare once told Zax she never wanted to be a pilot because of the pain surrounding her experience with two fellow cadets who lost their lives in a hull breach years earlier. She had initially swallowed her terror and entered the Pilot Academy to stand by her friend as he sought information about Mikedo's death. Her fears eventually receded, and Kalare ultimately stuck with the training because she developed a true fervor for it.

Why did Major Eryn have to make that comment about floating in space with your chair as a coffin? Kalare had experienced only passion for flying for months without a single twinge of apprehension.

She stood on the precipice of true flight. Fear would not invalidate her accomplishments.

Kalare fought to breathe deeply.

Success!

Again...

Success again!

The first two deep breaths were followed by three more and then her muscles finally unlocked. Kalare worried that her internal drama had lasted for mins and was noticed by all, but it had actually taken mere secs and almost everyone around the compartment had noticed nothing amiss. Except for Major Eryn. The major appraised Kalare knowingly, but the Omega's stoic look hid whatever feelings she might have. Kalare approached the technician.

"Cadet—please remove your clothes."

Kalare removed her pants and shirt to reveal the flight suit she had received yesterday. The suit was another piece of customized gear that optimized the interface between her body and the chair. She pulled its hood over her head and it adjusted against her scalp. A series of metal contact points were studded from the top of her skull to the base of her spine. A slight squeeze by the suit aligned all of them properly and prepared them to mate with the corresponding sensors in the chair. She was ready. She could do this. She sat in her chair and took one last deep breath.

The next sensation was beyond anything Kalare might have imagined. They had repeatedly simulated the process of transferring one's consciousness into a fighter during training, but the simulation was no substitute for the real thing. One moment Kalare was focused on the uncomfortable tightness of her flight suit around her neck, the next all traces of the suit had disappeared as if she was naked. The feeling was at once wildly disorienting and incredibly liberating. She somehow floated on air at the same time she was solidly grounded to the fighter which had sprung into existence beneath her.

A quick glance confirmed that everything was where she expected it to be in the cockpit, and she ran her preflight checklist. Her craft was green across the board. It was ready. She was ready. The voice of the Launch Controller broke the silence.

"Maverick—are you go for launch?"

Kalare replied, *"Maverick is go for launch."*

On those words a deep hum rumbled beneath the fighter, and Kalare recognized the EMALS spooling up. In a few secs she would be part of an impossibly fast projectile as the system electromagnetically launched her craft into space. The noise was a perfect match for the simulator, but the vibration it created in her virtual belly was wonderfully new.

Three.

Two.

One.

The immense rush of the EMALS shook Kalare to her core. Her body wasn't there, but nonetheless she experienced a sudden, intense acceleration that took her breath away. *This* is what it was like to be fired out the chamber of a gun! Starlight shone through the rapidly approaching launch portal ahead of her.

Now it was her turn.

Now she would fly.

CHAPTER FIFTEEN

Kalare's your friend, right?

Zax held his breath as the fighter shot out of the launch tube into space. His threat board labeled the craft with the pilot's call sign—Maverick. Kalare's call sign. Zax was both thrilled for his friend and wildly jealous that she got to experience the milestone first. The only positive aspect of being a year behind her at the Academy was they weren't competing directly. The top spot was available to both of them at the same time. He was lost for a moment thinking about the exhilaration and excitement she must be feeling until the Boss's voice dragged Zax back to Flight Ops.

"For those of you who might not be aware, Maverick today is none other than Cadet Kalare who runs Flight. I've worked with Kalare for the past year and it's great to see her first launch today as Maverick for her class."

The Boss cut in next over Zax's Plug.

"I hear congratulations are in order for you today as well, Zax. Major Eryn was quite shocked when you beat out that boy she's mentoring. Well done. There has never been any doubt you'd be great once you set your mind straight and got on the right path. You might be a little jealous that Kalare is out there first. Keep doing what you're doing, don't sabotage yourself again with anything silly, and it will be your turn soon enough."

Zax churned through a million possible replies. He kept it simple.

"Thank you, sir."

He began to stew over the Boss's dismissive reference to what had transpired between them a year earlier, but a sec later Zax's fuming was interrupted.

"Hey, cadet—why do I recognize the name Kalare?"

Was it really possible that Rege hadn't recognized he was working alongside another cadet he terrorized during the Revolution? He had been with her briefly that fateful day, but she was just one of the dozens of Crew held hostage in Engineering. They never used proper names in Flight Ops, only station names, so this was the first time her name had been spoken aloud in his presence.

When the civilian gave the order to kill Kalare months earlier, he had only known who she was because of Zax's reaction to hearing her name. He wouldn't make the same mistake this time. He stared blankly at Rege and shrugged his shoulders.

Zax returned his attention to the threat board. The fighters had launched, and the squadrons had dispersed to their separate rally points for their formation maneuvers. One of the pilots in Kalare's squadron was having a tough time adjusting and proved unable to hold a straight line. How was it possible for someone who had spent so much time in a simulator to look so bad once they were on the stick of an actual craft? Was the experience really that different given the immersiveness of the simulators?

"Of course! How could I forget? Kalare's your friend, right? The one I ordered killed right before the Boss handed everything over to us. She didn't die? How did I miss out on that interesting nugget of information?"

Zax's adrenalin spiked and he reacted on autopilot.

"Nope—she lived! Your goons did their best to kill a defenseless cadet, but they were unable to finish the job. What a shock considering the fine bunch of military geniuses you otherwise seemed to be!"

The insults hung between them. Rege stared at him impassively while Zax returned his gaze with defiance. He shouldn't reward the civilian with the satisfaction of getting under his skin. He had meekly suffered the man's barbs and insults for months and discretion suggested he should continue that approach.

Screw that! Zax was forced to swallow whatever the Boss dished out, but there was no good reason for him to turn away from the greasy civilian's abuse. He continued to stare the man down until an exclamation from Flight broke the spell.

"Boss—impact alert! Two birds collided at extreme velocity!"

A cloud of debris swirled on Zax's board, and he marveled at how the fighters involved in the crash had disintegrated. There were two fewer transponders broadcasting and that further signaled a serious crash. Collisions happened frequently enough with new pilots, but they usually sent the spacecraft involved back to the hangar for some minor repairs. Zax had never seen damage serious enough to silence one transponder much less two during a training exercise.

Wait—this was Kalare's squadron. One of the missing transponders was hers! Zax took a deep breath. He had to do his job.

"Boss—two transponders have gone dark." Zax sent an additional communication over their private channel. *"Sir—one of them is Kalare's."*

The Boss paused for a moment and then looked at Zax as he calmly spoke.

"OK, everyone. You know the drill. Get me a SAR bird out there ASAP. There's no way those two fighters collided so hard they damaged their cores. Let's get our pilots back safe and sound. Flight—while we wait for the search and rescue teams to retrieve the two cadets, please review what happened so we can figure out if one of them did something stupid enough to get dismissed from the Academy."

Zax appreciated the Boss's subtle reassurances about Kalare's safety. It was true that a training accident had never resulted in the death of a pilot while Zax had been involved with Flight Ops, but it was also accurate that he had never seen such a violent collision produce such destructive results. His heartbeat continued to accelerate and even the launch of the search and rescue craft failed to calm Zax's worries.

"Hey cadet—I know I'm still new to all of this complicated threat board stuff, and I'm sure no military genius, but I think I've managed to figure out which pilots were involved in that big old collision out there. One of them had the call sign Maverick. Isn't that the same call sign the Boss mentioned a few mins ago was your friend? What's her name again— Kalare?"

Rege stared at him with an expression which positively dripped malice. Zax struggled to retain his composure. The civilian would not get a rise out of him again. Zax turned away as Flight spoke to the compartment.

"Bad news, Boss. SAR found one of the cores and it was breached so we've got a KIA. Not sure which pilot it is yet. Stand by."

"What does a core breach mean, cadet? Isn't the core where the pilot's consciousness is stored? I thought I read somewhere that it's filled with some kind of biological material—like an artificial brain of

some sort. Does a breach mean one of those pilots was killed in action and her brain is leaking out into space? That sure sounds horrible, don't you think? Are you afraid it's your friend, Kalare? You must be sick with worry thinking it's your friend. Why are you turning red like that, cadet? Did I say something to make you upset? I'd hate if something I said made you upset."

Zax flew out of his chair and pushed the civilian out of his seat onto the deck. He stood over the man with his fists balled in white-knuckled fury. Rege met his eyes with a grin and didn't flinch as Zax raged at him over his Plug.

"I'm glad I killed your brother, you oxygen thief! That blade of yours was perfect for slipping into the back of his neck. You should have seen his eyes go wide as he clawed at his throat like there was something he could do to save himself!"

"Zax—stand down! You're dismissed. Return to your quarters. Scan—move to the threat board. No way I'm betting our safety on a rookie civilian."

Zax feared pressing his luck with the Boss yet again, but walking away was an admission of defeat. He continued to glare at Rege as the civilian's eyes narrowed to slits and his smug expression transformed into something different. Something much, much darker. After a few beats, Zax turned and stormed out of the compartment.

Why did he let the civilian get the better of him? And why did he lie about killing the man's brother? Zax had put himself directly into Rege's crosshairs for no good reason. He was fifty paces down the passageway and still chiding himself when a message came in from the Boss.

"Zax—they found Kalare's core. She's fine. I don't know what the hell that was between you and that civilian, but I'm disappointed you allowed him to get you worked up like that. Take the rest of the day to get your head straight and be certain you can prevent anything like that from ever happening again."

He wanted to scream. He wanted to call out the Boss for assigning Rege to be his mini. But Zax was determined to learn from losing control of his emotions and paused instead. The Omega might not even be aware of the history with Rege. After all, the officer hadn't been in the compartment when the civilian tormented Zax about the prospect of butchering Kalare. The man had no reason to know about Rege's behavior, so he most likely didn't. Zax took a final deep breath and replied as he prepared to enter the Tube.

"Yes, sir. My apologies for the inappropriate behavior, sir. It won't happen again."

CHAPTER SIXTEEN

I understand your predicament.

"Enter." Imair leaned back as the Boss came through the hatch. She gestured for him to take a seat and then closed her book and pushed it off to the side next to the half-eaten remains of her lunch and the bowl of fruit the stewards always kept full. He did a double-take when he noticed the book on the table and looked at her quizzically.

"What are you doing with that relic, ma'am?"

"I'm enjoying some ancient history."

"I understand how a book works, Madam President, and what one does with it. I'm surprised to find you handling ancient dead trees instead of using a slate."

"Interesting you should say that, Boss, as I'm surprised myself. I'm curious about what was happening back on Earth around the time the Ship was built. I've combed through our digital archives and can't find anything at all from that period of history. There's plenty of material that's even more ancient, like from the early twenty-first century, and tons of stuff from a few hundred years after the Ship's launch, but I can't find anything electronic that covers the years closest to the Ship's creation and the earliest parts of its journey. I had to have someone dig through the physical archives for the past couple of weeks just to find this one volume. It had been mis-shelved and was mixed in with a bunch of ancient religious texts."

"Those were difficult years, I imagine. I'm guessing that keeping historical records wasn't at the top of the priority list. At least, not quite as high priority as saving our species. Are you a big fan of studying history, ma'am?"

"I don't know if I'd call myself a fan, but I do believe you can learn an awful lot from what happened previously. My favorite quote is from one of Earth's most effective and influential statesmen. *Whoever wishes to foresee the future must consult the past.* There's a lot to be learned from that quote, Boss. Don't you agree?"

"If you say so, ma'am. I'm more inclined to look at what's happening around me rather than bury my nose in some musty old book."

Imair paused for a few moments to decipher whether there was any deeper meaning in the Boss's comment. She ultimately ignored it and instead segued into why she had summoned him.

"Speaking of seeing the future, Boss, I recall telling you months ago that making Rege work side-by-side with Zax was going to end poorly. I heard things got heated between them a few hours ago. Do you have any idea what happened? Can you help me understand once again what the hell you're thinking with that pairing? I explained their whole backstory months ago, and you jammed them together anyway."

The Boss took a deep breath. "Ma'am—my thinking was simple and I stand by it. There are two reasons for pushing Rege and Cadet Zax into such close proximity. The most important is that Rege is one of your most trusted lieutenants, and that's why you assigned him to Flight Ops. With that being true, I wanted him exposed to one of the most important positions on the Ship—running the threat board."

Imair wanted to grimace at the mention of Rege being a trusted lieutenant, but she tamped her emotions down and held her expression neutral. The young man had been a fantastic resource while they planned and executed the Revolution. Unfortunately, Rege's usefulness had dwindled in the months since. His default mode was to complain and agitate about her decisions and the compromises she was forced to make. He had valid points, particularly about the issues around living conditions for those civilians who weren't involved in leading and running the Ship, but his unwillingness to accept short-term tradeoffs for the sake of long-term success was infuriating. The Boss continued.

"The other reason for having the two of them work side-by-side is to force them to put aside their history in service to the bigger picture. Their peers know what has transpired between them. What better way to prove that we can all come back together and succeed than seeing two people who have so much enmity put aside their differences for the sake of the Ship."

Imair didn't want to admit publicly how Rege was causing her concern, so she had a hard time arguing the first of the Boss's points. He was absolutely right about his second reason, so she found herself in the same resigned position about the pairing as when she first raised her concerns. One thing still gnawed at her, though.

"OK, Boss, I'll support you keeping this in place. For now. If it escalates any further, we'll need to make adjustments so we don't trigger open warfare in Flight Ops. One thing is bothering me about Cadet Zax, though. From what I understand, he's clashed with you repeatedly. He's the one who ignored your orders and revealed the video about the human fighter. Hell—he tried to kill you rather than allow you to create a peaceful ending to the Revolution. Why are you continuing to support the boy and keep him around?"

The Boss stared at her for a few extra beats. Some unknown emotion flickered in his expression, but it disappeared before Imair pinned it down. He smiled instead, though one that was not the least bit genuine.

"The boy is extremely useful, ma'am."

Imair didn't understand the answer, but the Boss's tone suggested there wouldn't be anything further forthcoming.

"If you say so, Boss. Thanks for coming by. Dismissed."

The man stood and started to walk out but then stopped and turned back to Imair.

"One last thing, ma'am. Did I hear correctly there was some violence in one of the civilian sectors?"

Imair sighed. "Yes, it's incredibly frustrating. One of my key staff was down visiting family and was attacked on his way back to the Tube. It was originally only one crazy person, but something happened to get a larger crowd engaged and tearing things up. He got away without serious injury, but it was close."

"That's troubling, ma'am. And pretty surprising. Do you have any idea what's behind it?"

"I've been told we've got a group of agitators pushing us to move faster on the changes and improvements we're making. They're having a hard time understanding that things can't happen overnight. We've already increased civilian calorie allocation by 10 percent, and nutripellets are being distributed on a weekly basis to further augment rations. That's not good enough apparently. We've got a small group advocating that everyone should be allowed in Crew mess halls the same way critical civilian staff have been granted access. Can you imagine the chaos that would create? I feel really good about the progress we've made so far and I keep pushing the teams to get more done, but you know as well as anyone how much work we have to do to keep us moving toward finding those other humans."

The Boss smiled once again. "Yes, ma'am. You've got your mission identified and feel like you're making the tough leadership decisions necessary to support that mission. I understand your predicament. That sounds hard. Let me know if you would like any assistance. I've had some experience dealing with situations like that."

CHAPTER SEVENTEEN

I'll think about it.

W hen the evening newsvid ended, Zax turned to Kalare and sighed.

"I really don't like this announcer. I've given it three months, but I still can't get used to her. I wish the other guy was still around. I wonder why they got rid of him."

Kalare nodded. "I totally agree with you. She's not very likable, and I always feel like she's trying to convince me about something rather than just providing information. Well—at least she didn't have anything to say about me. It was a pretty boring news day given what they covered, so I kept worrying that a story about a couple of destroyed fighters might be newsworthy."

Pangs of jealousy left Zax conflicted when Kalare referenced her maiden flight. Even knowing it had almost been a disaster, he still found himself tipping toward upset about how she flew first. Yes—it had been Zax's choices and not Kalare's that put her on the path to beating him to the Academy by a year, but being a pilot had been his lifelong dream and for her was something she fell into. He fought to push his emotions aside and instead be a supportive friend.

"I can't believe that happened your very first time out there. What happened when they brought you back? What did Major Eryn have to say?"

It was Kalare's turn to sigh. "I'm so upset about the way she treated me. They had already completed the investigation by the time I was back on board and concluded there was nothing I could have done differently. It was entirely that idiot's fault. And yet, she starts screaming at me for making her look bad and hits me with a huge chunk of demerits."

"Wow—that sucks." Zax wasn't quite sure how to deal with Kalare's brewing emotions, so he changed the topic instead. "What was it like when you first saw your chair? Were you excited?"

Kalare paused for a moment. Zax worried he had somehow asked a bad question, but then her face brightened.

"I was thrilled to get in it! You can't believe what it's like, Zax. You spend all kinds of time getting tested and fitted. You finally get the flight suit on, and it's like you're going to be choked by the damn thing. But then you sit down in your chair and transfer into the fighter. And...wow. All I can say is wow. The power of the EMALS. Did you know you can actually feel it in your stomach? Then...finally...you're in space. Nothing between you and death except a few nanometers of reinforced titanium. You know your body really isn't there, but somehow you still feel like it totally is. At one point I swear I scratched an itch on my knee! I thought it would be more scary when my fighter got destroyed and my core got ejected, but it happened so many times when I was flying with you in your simulator that I was totally prepared for it. Sorry if that comes across as an insult in any way, but it's not meant to."

Kalare acted even more manic than usual during her retelling, but Zax smiled regardless. Someone walked up behind her and his grin faded when he lifted his gaze to discover it was Mase. The boy had a tray of food in his hand and pointed at one of the two empty seats at their table.

"Can I sit down?"

Zax wanted to say no, but curiosity about what the young cadet was after got the better of him and he nodded instead. The boy sat with his back to Kalare and spoke to Zax.

"I've got to know how you beat me in the simulator. You have no business being that good your first day."

Zax should have expected it given what he already knew about the boy, but the complete lack of social grace was surprising nonetheless. He was far from perfect when it came to human interaction, but Mase took Zax's quirks and amplified them by a factor of ten. Zax replied.

"I could ask you the same question. You were a little too smooth out there."

"It wasn't my first time. The Major gave me introductory sessions last week. I will deny it if you ever tell anyone."

The boy smiled with great self-satisfaction in sharing his news. Zax was incensed. He turned to Kalare, who shared his look of disbelief, and then back to the boy.

"What? That's against regulations! All Pilot Academy cadets are supposed to be kept on equal footing at all times and be provided with the same opportunities for simulator time, training sessions, etc."

"Don't blame me. Was I supposed to say no when she offered? I answered your question. You haven't answered mine. What's your story? How are you cheating?"

Zax wanted to tell the boy to slag off but instead sought to take him down a notch.

"I built my own simulator so I've been practicing for almost a year."

Mase shook his head.

"That doesn't make sense. I've seen flight games other people created. They can't provide what it takes to become a pilot. Only Academy simulators prepare you."

Zax was sorting out how best to disprove Mase's assertion when Kalare jumped into the conversation.

"Yes—lots of kids have built lots of stupid simulators. Zax built an amazing one. I'm a year ahead of you two, and his simulator is absolutely as good as the ones in the Academy. And almost as realistic as flying. Except the EMALS. I told you about the EMALS, right, Zax? About how you can feel it in your belly? But anyway, Zax's simulator is definitely as amazing and useful as the ones at the Academy. Before you walked up, in fact, we were talking about how I wasn't afraid when I crashed today and my core got ejected because it happened so many times when Zax and I were using his simulator. If I were you, I would—"

Mase put his palm in front of Kalare's face to cut her off. "Do you have an off switch?"

Kalare reacted as if she was genuinely confused and hurt by the boy's question and his tone. Something fierce welled up within Zax and he glared at Mase.

"Leave her alone!"

The cadet put both of his hands palm out toward Zax in a non-threatening, conciliatory fashion.

"No harm intended. It made me tired trying to keep up with her."

"Hey, Puke Boy. Hey, Kalare."

Aleron had appeared and sat down in the fourth chair while Zax was focused on Mase. Kalare had mentioned the Engineering cadet with alarming regularity in the months since the Revolution, but Zax had thankfully avoided any interactions with him.

Aleron's tone was friendly when he used the dreaded nickname, but Zax was already primed for upset and his adrenalin surged. Aleron looked at Mase for a moment without any recognition before turning back to Kalare and putting his hand on her arm.

"I heard about what happened to you. That's crazy! Are you OK? Can you tell me about it?"

Zax went to stand and pushed his chair backward with a little more force than he intended. It toppled over and crashed to the floor. He ignored it and balled up his nutripellet wrappers.

"I've got to go. I've got work to do. Goodbye."

Kalare called after him. "Zax—wait. Don't go."

Zax kept his head down and charged toward the waste bins. Footsteps raced up from behind him, and he debated what he would say to Kalare when she caught up.

"Puke Boy—that's you?"

It was Mase, not Kalare. Zax sped up, but the young Zeta kept pace despite being a half-meter shorter than Zax.

"I wondered why you were eating nutripellets. You're a legend. There are permanent stains in the Zeta berth that people say are yours. I can't believe it's you."

Leave it to a fourteen-year-old to think someone would be excited at being recognized for their vomiting prowess. Zax stopped short and spun to face the boy.

"What do you want? Why are you following me?"

"I want you to show me your simulator. If it's any good, I want to practice in it with you. You've got a big head start on flying. You'll probably always be better than me. In exchange, I'll share special tricks for succeeding on the Leaderboard."

Zax was dumbfounded. This kid had just admitted his mentor was cheating to give him an advantage, and now he was asking Zax to help make him even better yet. His initial instinct was to scream *no* and run in the other direction, but he forced himself to consider the situation for a moment. Clearly this kid was smart and knew a thing or two about how to succeed. Maybe it was a good idea to take advantage of the boy's skill and boost himself even higher on the Leaderboard in the process. Zax was confident that, unless he allowed Mase to spend every waking moment in the simulator, the boy would never catch up to his flight skills. What, then, was the risk in trading off to support each other? There had to be something he wasn't taking into account, so Zax left the door open without committing.

"I'll think about it. Now seriously—I've got work to do, so leave me alone."

CHAPTER EIGHTEEN

Well played, Adan.

"**M**arkev—get off him! You're killing him!" Adan clawed at his bodyguard's massive shoulders in a vain attempt to stop the man's pummeling of the hangar attendant. Markev reached back and gave his boss a casual shove that sent Adan tumbling away end over end in the microgravity environment. Markev delivered one last vicious kick to the attendant's skull, and then the giant oriented himself toward their temporary quarters and kicked off against the bulkhead to glide in that direction. The attendant's eyes were already swollen nearly shut and globules of blood oozed from a cut on his face, but the man retained enough of his senses to push off and float on a wobbly path toward the medic station.

It had happened in an instant. They landed their FTL test craft and were in the process of disembarking when the attendant said something under his breath. Markev jumped at him and sent them both flying toward a bulkhead. As they came to rest against it, Markev had grabbed a handhold and used it to keep his body positioned such that he kept the defenseless man pinned against the wall with a cascade of punishing kicks and punches.

What had caused Markev to snap and rage? He was a fierce operator which is why Adan had hired him in the first place, but in their decades together the man had never lost his cool even in the face of some challenging situations. Their current pace of work was arduous, but it wasn't anything worse than projects they had been involved in previously. Adan was out of sorts and short-tempered, but he expected exhaustion from himself. Not from the indefatigable Markev.

The good news was that after two dozen test flights over three days, Adan was finally convinced they had created a reliable FTL engine capable of powering a craft big enough for dozens of people. He still had significant worries about whether the design would scale up to the level necessary to instantly transport his asteroid across the universe, but that was a challenge to deal with down the road.

The challenge that sat right in front of him was his regular status call with Earth. He usually delivered his updates to the Chancellor's technical staff who understood and appreciated what he had to share with them. His next call would be with the Chancellor herself, however, along with her Chief of Staff. Adan appreciated that he needed to keep playing the political game for a few more years while the project moved forward. This was particularly true given the value of the Chancellor dedicating the West's resources to the cause. That understanding didn't prevent the process from feeling quite annoying. He had so many crucial projects reaching critical stages of development that every moment taken away from them risked delaying the mission.

Adan glided across the hangar toward the temporary command facility. The massive space had been one of the first projects completed, and it had been a hive of activity throughout the two years since. They were within weeks of the first groundbreaking for a surface tower, so the level of bustle had only amped up even further. Everything was tracking more or less according to plan, but the mining was always going to be the easiest part of the project.

Adan arrived at the conference room and settled in just as an image from the Chancellor's office materialized on the screen. A minute later, the woman and her Chief of Staff sat down in front of the camera. The Chancellor appeared serene and content, while Jania emanated her usual agitation. The leader of the West spoke first.

"Good afternoon, Adan. How are you doing today?"

"I'm doing fine, Madam Chancellor. Thank you for asking. How are things down there?"

"Well, to be honest, they've been better. We'll get to that a little later, though. I'd like to hear from you first. I've been getting regular updates, but I'd love to get an unfiltered summary from you."

"My pleasure, ma'am. An awful lot has happened up here since that first time I visited your office, but I'll try to cover what I think are the high points.

"The mining operation has gone tremendously well, as expected. We've extracted sufficient titanium for all of the construction within the interior of the asteroid as well as enough for a much larger number of surface structures than we had originally envisioned. There have been astounding improvements made in our ability to extract titanium from the ore, and we've even managed to adapt the techniques for transparent aluminum to create transparent titanium which is orders of magnitude stronger. We'll start putting all of that titanium to use and breaking ground on our first surface structure within the next two weeks.

"We've also made great progress thanks to the white dwarf's degenerate gas that you provided. I'm pleased to report that just a few minutes ago I returned from my twenty-fourth test flight of the new faster-than-light engine. We've actually used our test flights to source more of the gas from Sirius B, so we now have sufficient fuel to complete all of our development work. The final step will be to scale the FTL technology up to an engine than can move something as massive as the completed spaceship."

Adan didn't feel it was prudent to inform the Chancellor about his worries on that front, so he jumped ahead.

"The last major area of development encompasses some of the new systems that are critical to maximize the success of the mission. Once again, we have your extreme generosity with regards to the degenerate gas to thank for our progress."

Adan found it distasteful to stroke the Chancellor's ego quite so vigorously, but he had been told by many that it worked. He continued.

"Artificial gravity and inertial dampening are two technologies that go hand in hand from an engineering perspective. Our recent breakthroughs have come thanks to the energy characteristics of the degenerate gas. I expect to have some groundbreaking developments in these areas within the next year based on the pace of results so far."

Jania appeared dubious. "Will you guarantee that timeline for the artificial gravity, Adan? That technology has always struck me as an absolute requirement if you're going to have people living for a century on this spaceship of yours."

Adan shook his head slowly. "I think you know better than to ask a question like that." He turned to the Chancellor. "Ma'am, I've been financing this operation entirely on my own to date, and I'm well prepared to do so until it is complete. If you folks are going to start pressuring me for guarantees, perhaps you would consider putting some skin in the game yourselves. If you are worried about the timeline and my progress, would you like to make some additional resources available that will help us accelerate the pace?"

The Chancellor smiled. "Well played, Adan. Jania has still not quite developed her father's patience, and her comment about guarantees clearly showed more of my hand than I would've hoped. There are two fronts down here on which I'm battling where I feel we're facing dwindling time horizons.

"First, the East has become more and more belligerent about your project. Even though you're acting as a private citizen, they're trying to make the case that all of the resources you're pouring into the spaceship are violating the spirit of our climate treaty with them. They want me to nationalize your wealth and direct everything back toward saving the Earth rather than fleeing it. I know that so far we've left the topic of slots for citizens of the East as an item we'll discuss as we get closer to departure, but we may need to start that negotiation process sooner than later."

Already being on edge from his exhaustion, any suggestion of compromising with the East threatened to derail Adan altogether. He nodded to acknowledge the comment and focused on breathing deeply without allowing his displeasure to show too much. The Chancellor continued.

"The more worrisome development down here is the state of the climate itself. I have a secret group sequestered near what's left of Antarctica. They have access to the best data available about what's happening around the globe. Over the last six months, they've seen a rapid acceleration of climate decay. Whereas we previously believed we had a century or more, their new models are suggesting we might be lucky to get a decade or two before we tip into unsurvivable catastrophe."

Adan was not taken aback by this news as his models had long suggested the same. That was why he was dedicating every ounce of his fortune into completing the spaceship as quickly as possible. His breathing had brought his anger under control, and he replied confidently.

"Madam Chancellor—conscript me the group of scientists and engineers from the list I will provide you, and I will absolutely guarantee we'll get this done within the next thirty months."

The woman nodded and the screen went blank as the connection was terminated. Adan smiled. He would have finished within thirty months anyway, but now he had guaranteed himself access to a brilliant team. The people on his list would complete the docket of intellects he envisioned as an ideal crew to launch the ship once it was ready. He would have convinced most of them to join him regardless, but it sure was easier to just have the government force them on a shuttle and deliver them.

An engine throttled up out in the hangar, and Adan turned to watch through the panorama. It reminded him that he wanted to update the blueprints and move the flight operations center to a different location. Being able to view both the inside of the hangar and outside into space from the same compartment would likely be a useful design feature down the road.

CHAPTER NINETEEN

Why are they firing at us, Z?

"*Z—form up closer on me. They're watching to see how we perform. Don't make us look bad!*"

Zax wanted to tell Mase it was his own damn fault they were breaking formation because the younger boy always drifted off line by the smallest fraction. He held back as he replied.

"*Aye-aye, Prime. Though I'm guessing the Boss probably doesn't pay too much attention to routine Combat Air Patrols.*"

No sooner did they have this discussion than Mase drifted even further off course. Zax was debating the most appropriate way to tell the boy to get his act together when an alarm warbled and an FTL bloom materialized on his threat board. Then five more. Then twenty more. He keyed his communicator.

"Flight—are you seeing this?"

"Affirmative. Threat reports twenty-six inbound bogeys of unknown origin. The Alert Two birds will join up with you in one hundred and forty secs. Establish visual contact and report."

Mase accelerated his fighter toward the bogeys, and Zax matched his speed and heading. Fifty secs later they were within visual range, and Zax heard Mase gasp.

"Z—are you seeing what I'm seeing? They're all just like the fighter from that planet. It's the other humans. We've found them!"

A reply died on Zax's lips as his threat board erupted with warnings about weapons being fired at his fighter. He hailed the Ship.

"Flight—we've identified the inbounds. Prime and I concur they match the human fighter that was discovered previously, but they're coming in hot. Do we have permission to engage the bandits?"

"Red Squadron—do not engage. You are not weapons free. Repeat, you are not weapons free. Evade, but maintain visual contact and report your observations. The Alert Two's are inbound your position with ETA seventy secs. Comms is hailing the bandits and ordering them to stand down."

"Prime—watch your six!"

Mase reacted to Zax's warning and juked his fighter away from an incoming plasma bolt. Another dozen human craft had jumped into the system directly behind them and immediately fired. The boy called out to Zax with desperation in his voice.

"Why are they firing at us, Z? Shouldn't it be obvious we're human? Our spacecraft are so similar. Shouldn't they be curious and not shoot?"

"I don't have a clue, Prime. I'm just trying to stay alive!"

Another alarm wailed, but this one was different and Zax involuntarily opened his eyes. Crew scattered in every direction around the mess hall while the alert for General Quarters blared. Mase had exited the simulation as well, and Zax grinned at the boy and then bolted toward Flight Ops. Mase contacted him via his Plug.

"Really, Zax? Human fighters? I thought we had an agreement. You're supposed to help me with your simulations—not play make-believe!"

"Relax, OK. It was a good test. Or was that not complete terror I heard in your voice right at the end? The point of a simulation is to create entirely extreme situations so all of the everyday stuff becomes routine. You really shouldn't feel that bad since this is the worst you've failed in the three months we've done this. You'll do better next time. At least I hope so. Besides, you still haven't bothered to show me any of your tricks to help with the Leaderboard."

The truth was that Zax didn't really worry about learning Mase's tricks since he remained on top of the Theta Leaderboard as he always had. He enjoyed needling the boy, though. They were never going to be friends, particularly because of the way Mase and Kalare rubbed each other wrong, but Zax enjoyed working alongside the young cadet more than he did 99.9 percent of the other people in the Crew. Mase laughed.

"In good time, Zax. In good time. What do you think this alert is about? Did the scout ship get attacked?"

"Can't be that or else we'd be at Condition Two, right? My guess is the Boss is just feeling a little antsy about returning to a colony for the first time. Or maybe he's worried a bunch of human fighters are going to jump out of FTL and attack us. I sure hope he handles it better than you did."

"Nice one. You really got me there, Zax. Have fun in Flight Ops."

Zax reached his seat and took over for one of the secondary Threats who worked the board when Zax was elsewhere. Rege arrived fifty secs later and slipped on his subvoc. He pinged Zax on their private channel.

"What's going on, cadet? I thought today was only a scouting mission."

"I have no idea. The alert goes off and I run. Wait—here's the Boss."

"I've called General Quarters because the scout ship we sent to evaluate the colony prior to our arrival in system tomorrow has missed their rendezvous time. I'm going to give them another thirty mins, and then I'm sending a larger force to evaluate the situation.

"Flight—prepare a SAR party that includes both air and ground assets. If they've crashed or otherwise landed on the planet, we may need to extract them.

"Everyone else—I want you alert for anything. Who knows what we might find nearly one hundred years after we left this colony behind."

Not even a sec later Rege was back on their private channel.

"Hey cadet—I'm confused. I was alive when we dropped these folks off. What's the Boss talking about when he says one hundred years?"

"Have you ever heard about the concept of time dilation?"

The civilian shook his head, and Zax sighed at the prospect of having to explain something so complex to a civilian. He was about to risk the man's ire by telling him he just wouldn't understand when the threat board demanded his attention and he escaped the discussion.

"Boss—FTL bloom. It's coming in to the rendezvous coordinates. I've confirmed its signature and the bird is ours."

"Flight—I want that pilot on my panorama, and I want her up there now!"

A moment later the pilot of the scout craft was displayed on the exterior panorama. She appeared momentarily taken aback when she recognized she was being broadcast to the entire compartment, but she recovered quickly and spoke.

"My apologies, Boss, for our delayed return. There are no humans. Anywhere. We didn't believe what the sensors and drones were showing, so we decided to take a few extra mins for a surface pass to see for ourselves. We didn't land, but we got plenty low enough to confirm the colonists up and left without any struggle whatsoever. Their colony had grown beyond the original boundaries, but most of the original facilities were still present and appear exactly the way they do in the imagery archive."

The Boss paused like he was deep in thought, and he chomped on his cigar more furiously than Zax had ever seen. He finally replied.

"This changes everything. This plan is pending final approval from President Imair, but I want everyone moving it forward now.

"First, I want all of the sensor imagery from that scout craft on my slate within the next fifteen mins. I want the pilot and crew in my conference room fifteen mins after that. We're sending a group to the surface to pore over this colony for any clues about what might have happened, and I'm going to lead it myself. I want a team from Engineering to inspect and evaluate all of the mechanical systems the colony left behind. I'm also going to need a team who can extract all of their data archives and transfer them to Alpha for further processing. And, of course, I'm going to need a security detail just in case something is not as it appears."

The Boss gazed around the room for a min before he continued.

"You all must remain absolutely focused on keeping this Ship safe. I have no idea what might be going on, but something doesn't feel right. This might be a trap, but given our new mission it's a trap we have no choice but to risk triggering."

The Boss removed the cigar from his mouth and placed it in his shirt pocket as he turned and exited the compartment. Flight Ops was as silent as always, but there was an electricity in the air that usually only existed when the Ship prepared for an alien encounter. Kalare pinged Zax a min later.

"Zax—you're not going to believe the message I just got! The Boss wants me to have an opportunity to fly a surface mission, so he's ordered Major Eryn to pilot his shuttle tomorrow with me as her co-pilot. Can you believe it? I'm going to the surface! I sure hope no one tries to kill me this time."

CHAPTER TWENTY

How cool is that?

The presence of the Boss and Sergeant Bailee on the flight deck added significantly to the stress that Kalare experienced sitting in the right seat next to Major Eryn. The head of the Academy clearly lacked enthusiasm about sharing the piloting duties with Kalare and had made her displeasure obvious in both word and tone from the first moment they discussed the mission parameters. Her negative attitude was never more apparent than when she "coached" Kalare on her control of the shuttle.

"Cadet—what did I tell you about the angle of attack as we enter the atmosphere? You're off optimal glide slope by half a percent. Are you capable of doing this the way you've been instructed, or should I take the stick back?"

Kalare made the adjustment. The blood rushed to her cheeks as she worried about how the Boss might react to her mistakes. She held her breath when he picked that moment to reach out over her Plug.

"Don't mind her, Kalare. She's more displeased about me dragging her along on this trip than anything to do with you. You're flying well considering you haven't graduated yet. No wonder you've been Maverick for so much of your time in the Academy."

Kalare wanted to grin but feared incurring the wrath of the major.

"Thank you, sir. And thank you once again for the opportunity to make this trip today."

The Boss next spoke aloud.

"Thank you, Major. I was wondering if you were going to bother saying anything or whether perhaps I was the only one who had noticed."

"Yes, sir. My apologies."

Kalare again fought to keep her face neutral. She had no idea why the Boss was tweaking Eryn the way he was, but it sure was fun to watch. Kalare fretted about how the major might take her frustrations out on her, but she trusted the Boss knew how far to push.

A few mins later the shuttle pierced the cloud deck and the colony appeared off in the distance. Its drab gray buildings stood out in stark relief to the yellow of the surrounding vegetation. Sergeant Bailee spoke.

"Sir—may I suggest we do a few low-level passes to get a full visual of the colony and its surroundings? I've studied all of the sensor data and drone footage, but I'd like to see it with my own eyes if that's OK with you."

"I agree, Sergeant. Cadet—drop to five hundred meters, circumnavigate the colony twice, cross over it once from north to south, and again from east to west. Unless we see anything strange, set us down on the landing pad next to the main administration center."

"Aye-aye, Boss." Kalare had assumed the major would take control of the shuttle once they neared the colony and was thrilled when the Boss explicitly directed her to remain on the stick instead. Eryn was visible out of the corner of her eye, and the woman's body language suggested significant displeasure with the situation.

What stood out the most to Kalare as they surveyed the colony was how its core matched the one she had visited with Zax. This colony had outgrown its initial boundaries and expanded outwards, but its heart was Ship standard for design and construction.

The colony checked out as clear from the air, so she landed the shuttle on the pad next to the main administration center as she had been instructed. Sergeant Bailee left to prepare the security squad, and the Boss turned to Kalare before he followed.

"Great landing, cadet. You're a shining testament to the instruction that Major Eryn and her team are imparting at the Academy. If only all of our officers were doing such a superlative job in their respective areas."

The Boss turned and left the flight deck without waiting for any reply from the major. Kalare had feared the worst in anticipating the woman's behavior toward her once they were alone, but the Boss's parting compliment had the effect she assumed the man intended. After a brief but self-satisfied grin, the major turned and addressed Kalare.

"Well done, cadet. Generally the pilots remain on board while the landing party does their work, but the Boss has directed that you be allowed to exit the shuttle and view the colony along with his squad. Dismissed."

Kalare was thrilled about her good fortune. She had assumed she would be stuck spending the next few hours waiting in awkward silence alongside the major. She opened a channel to Zax to share the news as she walked through the shuttle.

"Hey, Zax—you're never going to believe this! They're letting me off the shuttle, so I can check out the colony with the Boss. How cool is that?"

"Wow, Kalare, that's great. What's it like down there?"

"You saw that other colony, so you've pretty much seen this one too. They look the same. The only difference is the flora on this planet is nothing like it was on that other one. Everything is a pale yellow and there isn't a single piece of vegetation that's taller than a meter. Wait a sec—I'll be right back with you."

Kalare had exited the shuttle and was surprised to see a familiar face in a red Engineering uniform. Aleron must have ridden down in the other shuttle. She called out to him.

"Hey there! What are you doing here?"

"I was about to ask you the same thing! They brought me down to help evaluate the state of the colony's systems. You?"

"The Flight Boss had me pilot his shuttle down. Now I'm heading to join up with his squad to check out the colony. Uh-oh...looks like I might be late."

Sergeant Bailee approached from behind Aleron. The cadet had no idea the man was there and nearly fell to the ground when the Marine intentionally bumped against him on his way past. He stopped and appraised Aleron with withering disdain.

"Well if it isn't Captain Clueless himself. You'll be happy to know, *sir*, that I have it on good authority there aren't any rodents on this planet. Nothing to be afraid of—you're safe. Though, you won't be for long if you don't double-time it and catch up to the rest of the engineers. They're about to head out without you, and I don't think you really want to spend any time with me instead of them."

Aleron's cheeks flushed almost a shade darker than his uniform, and he turned and hustled away without a further word. The Marine addressed her with the slightest smile creasing his mouth.

"Cadet—we're ready to head out. Follow me."

Kalare fell into step behind the Marine and contacted Zax again.

"Sorry about that. I ran into Aleron. I had no idea he was coming down here too! You would've loved it. Sergeant Bailee reminded him about his screw-up from the maintenance tunnels, and he went running away with his tail between his legs."

There was an uncomfortable silence. Kalare would have imagined Zax would be thrilled to hear about Bailee tormenting Aleron, but once again her friend reacted negatively to the simple mention of the engineering cadet's name. She really needed to get to the bottom of his issues, but Zax always shut her down whenever she broached the topic. She wanted to be compassionate as she knew he had been through a lot, but she was approaching the end of her patience around it all. Zax finally replied.

"I hope everything goes well down there. Don't get into any trouble, OK? I've got to get going."

"Sure thing, Zax. Unless we find anything interesting, I think the plan is that we'll be back in time for dinner. I'll see you then and tell you all about it!"

Zax cut the connection without another word. Kalare put her frustration with him aside and smiled at the Boss as she approached.

"Sir—thank you for allowing me to accompany you."

"Sure thing, cadet. Stay close, OK? If anything unexpected happens, I want you near Bailee."

"Yes, sir."

The Boss turned and strode toward the main administration building. Kalare followed and Bailee fell into formation behind her. They were joined by three other Marines. At least, three who were visible. Kalare had been hearing rumors the Boss had a new and ever-present security detail cloaked in ChamWare, and she was determined to catch a sign of their presence if they really existed.

What struck her most as they walked was the stillness around them. There was no wind whatsoever and no noise other than the crunch of the dirt under their feet. The air smelled as sterile as it did on the Ship, though it carried far more heat and humidity. Beads of perspiration formed on her brow and her shirt clung uncomfortably to the small of her back.

They reached the entrance of the administration building, and one of the Marines checked a slate before addressing Bailee.

"Sergeant—sensors confirm no movement and no signs of life inside. Do you want us to verify the building is clear before the Boss enters?"

The Boss jumped in before Bailee had a chance to reply.

"Stand down, Marine. This place is deader than dead, so let's not waste any more time than we absolutely must chasing ghosts. I want to find anything worthwhile, and then get out of here as fast as we can."

Bailee nodded in what came across as reluctant agreement, and they all entered. The most extraordinary thing to Kalare about the interior was that nothing was out of the ordinary. Everything inside the building was as boring and normal as everything else around the colony. It was as if the colonists had stood up in the middle of a work shift and left with nothing but the clothes on their back. At the Boss's direction she dug through drawer after drawer for anything of interest, but everywhere she searched revealed nothing but the same, boring detritus of normal life.

The Boss called them all together a short time later. He confirmed that no one had found anything of interest and sighed.

"Well, that makes us just like the other teams then. Let's get back to the shuttles and get off this rock. I have no idea what might have happened here, but there's nothing to learn by staying any longer. We've got all of their data systems. Perhaps Alpha can find something interesting by sifting through their electronic records."

Kalare gave one last look around before she exited the building. The longer they stayed, the creepier the absolute normalcy became, so she was happy to head back to the Ship. As they walked back she smelled something odd. She turned and found that the tip of the Boss's cigar glowed red and he was blowing smoke out of his mouth. The thing stank in an indescribably foul manner, and she found herself wildly grateful for the Ship's regulations which prohibited the man from lighting it up more often.

They reached the shuttles and found they were the last team to return. The Boss asked Kalare to wait for a quick word before boarding.

"I hope you enjoyed this chance to get off the Ship, Kalare. I have big plans for your future that might well involve more missions like this, so it was great to see your comfort and composure down here. Some people have a hard time dealing with being out in the open on a planet after a lifetime cooped up on the Ship."

"It was fantastic, sir. Thanks again for allowing me to come along. I'll look forward to doing it again, though I just hope next time there's more interesting things to see and do."

The Boss exhaled one last cloud of acrid smoke and then tossed the remains of his cigar to the ground as he grinned.

"Be careful what you wish for, cadet."

CHAPTER TWENTY-ONE

You're correct, Boss.

"Boss—we've burned a month and visited a dozen colonies and every one has been the same. The colonists on each planet have disappeared without a trace and without any signs of a struggle. Alpha has reviewed all of their data systems but reports everything has been purged so there are no electronic records. What the hell do you think is going on?"

Imair pounded the table repeatedly in sync with her question. The shaking knocked a couple of pieces of fruit off the top of the bowl that was always there, and the Boss placed them back as he answered.

"I don't know, Madam President. It makes zero sense to me. These colonies have all been among our more recent ones, but the amount of local time which has elapsed since settlement has differed by hundreds of years. There shouldn't be any commonality between them other than being relatively near each other—at least on a cosmic scale. The only thing I find interesting is that all of them have been lower quality planets."

Imair furrowed her brow. "Lower quality planets? What do you mean by that?"

"Throughout the Ship's history, we've applied a quality scale to each habitable planet we've discovered. We rank them from one to ten with regards to how attractive they are from a settlement perspective. There are a number of criteria we consider that factor into the final score, but it all boils down to how well the planet will support human life. The scale has been calibrated where a planet identical to Earth would rank as an eight—pretty attractive, but there have been numerous planets over time that were even better."

"OK—you said these have all been lower quality. What does that mean? Did they all rank as ones?"

The Boss shook his head. "No, ma'am. A one is a planet where life is sustainable, but barely. We've settled a few of those in history, but only in times of significant distress where the Ship had not made Landfall for long periods of time. When the Ship first launched, their goal was to leave colonies on planets that scored a six or better. Over time, as the Crew realized the scarcity of habitable worlds, that shifted until three became the accepted threshold below which we would generally not settle. This group we have visited have been mostly fours and fives with one six in there."

Imair contemplated the explanation for a few min. The Boss watched her with a neutral expression.

"That's an interesting coincidence, Boss. I'm curious. Do we have any colonies that rank significantly higher and align with our present course back to Earth?"

"I had a feeling you might react that way, ma'am. There is a system where the planet meets both of those criteria. It was rated a nine, and if we were to head straight there at our current pace of Transits, we would reach it in approximately eleven months. Shall we set that course right now?"

Imair shook her head. "No. Let's go ahead and check out the next colony on our list tomorrow as planned. If we have the same experience there as we've had at all of the others, then let's head straight to the planet that rated a nine. Would you suggest anything different?"

"No, ma'am. That's what I would recommend. There's one thing I'm curious about, if I may. Perhaps I've missed it, but I haven't heard any mention of the abandoned colonies on any of the newsvids. Is that accurate?"

Imair had been waiting for the man to call her out on this topic and was fairly shocked it had taken this long.

"You're correct, Boss. We've intentionally withheld that information from wider broadcast. I'm sure rumors are spreading fast enough that trying to hide the news doesn't make sense any longer, but my civilian advisors have counseled withholding it as the safest course of action."

"Why is that, ma'am? Aren't you afraid you'll lose your credibility with the civilian population when they discover you've been lying to them?"

Imair grimaced. "Only every moment of every day. This has been my hardest decision since taking this role. Let's be clear that we aren't actually lying, though. I want transparency so everyone on the Ship understands what is happening with our journey, but I've gotten spooked by the amount of violence in the civilian sectors. If people hear that a Mission we pursued for 5,000 years is essentially a failure because every single colony has died, then it may destroy whatever final vestige of hope they're nursing about our situation."

"I understand that rationalization, Madam President. I will offer that lies of omission are generally evaluated the same as lies of commission when the truth comes out. And it always comes out. What are you worried about, ma'am, another uprising?"

"I realize it may sound absurd given your current situation, Boss, but there are far worse outcomes for the Ship and the Crew than what has happened after my Revolution. There are large swaths of the civilian population who argued for putting every single one of you out an airlock. You may not be thrilled about my leadership, but I can promise you'll be less thrilled if you were to lose me and instead face some of the more radical civilian elements."

Imair knew the Boss was already dealing with at least one of the more radical elements in the form of Rege, but she didn't want to hold him up as a negative example and thereby clue the Boss in to her true feelings about the dangerous civilian. As she tried to convince the Boss that her team was the most reasonable alternative to Crew rule, positioning Rege in his mind as someone who still qualified as "reasonable" was useful. The Boss appeared dubious about her explanation, but it wasn't her job to convince the man. It was her job to maintain the fragile peace and that by itself required every ounce of her energy.

"Thanks for the counsel, Boss. And thanks for sharing your opinion about my approach with the civilians. Even though I may not agree with your assessment, I appreciate hearing it. What's the plan for this next colony?"

"We'll send out the scout shuttle shortly to scan the planet in advance of us jumping there tomorrow. Assuming it is like the rest, we'll send a ground team to look up close and extract their data systems. Recent history suggests there won't be anything on them, but we should be certain. Is there anything you would like to do differently?"

There were many things that Imair wanted to do differently, but for now she was stuck on the path she had chosen. She shook her head.

"No, that sounds great. Thank you. Dismissed."

CHAPTER TWENTY-TWO

We all have our little hobbies.

Reveille droned on and on and on. Zax ignored it and instead lounged in his bunk for an extended period (twenty demerits). He had increasingly lost interest in getting out of bed as the Ship discovered empty colony after empty colony. He hadn't expected they would find the other humans anytime too soon, but he despaired a full decade of nutripellets if they continued at this rate.

He shuffled to the showers and took one that was both extra hot (twenty demerits) and extra long (twenty more demerits). The extended soak didn't soothe his mood, and his mindset got even worse when he glanced at the Theta Leaderboard on his way to breakfast. He was no longer in first place! Zax had been so focused on what was going on at the Academy that he had not paid attention to the Theta standings for weeks. His scoring cushion had evaporated, and sixty new demerits were sufficient to push him into second place! He knew he shouldn't care about being number one since he had already gotten into the Academy, but he was vexed nonetheless.

Zax dragged himself to the mess hall and grabbed "breakfast" from the dispenser. He considered tempting fate and eating real food instead of nutripellets, but he ultimately refrained. He was scheduled to work Flight Ops during the Transit to the next colony and wanted to maintain his streak of a puke-free threat board. He immediately regretted the decision to not medicate his depression with food when he found Mase at their table instead of Kalare.

"Zax—Kalare had to check in with Aleron about something. She said she couldn't wait for you any longer."

It was the perfect capstone to a crappy morning. Kalare had gone off with that oxygen thief yet again, and Zax had to hear the news from Mase. He slammed his nutripellets on to the table and flopped his body into a chair while choking back a scream. He knew it was an absurd overreaction to the situation, but that didn't tame his response.

The young Zeta observed Zax's response to the mention of Aleron and then smiled. "Wow—you must really have a thing for her. I didn't realize messing with you would have this much of an effect. She's not off with Aleron. She had to take care of something at the

Academy. She felt bad she would miss you this morning. I wouldn't have joked around if I had known it would upset you so much."

Zax fought the urge to strike Mase. One deep breath after another finally calmed Zax sufficiently that he no longer risked falling even further down the Leaderboard due to hitting another cadet. Mase continued.

"What's got you so worked up? I hope it isn't just my joke."

"No—it's not just you. I was already pretty angry walking in here, and your little joke was the final straw. I woke up feeling pretty crappy, and then discovered how I managed to drop myself into second place on the Theta Leaderboard by lounging in bed and then taking too long and too hot of a shower."

The boy smiled. "I'm sorry for piling on to your bad mood. How about I make good on our trade to make it up to you?" Mase closed his eyes and focused on his Plug for a min. "Check your ranking now."

Zax closed his eyes. The sixty demerits he had been assessed since waking had been removed and he was at the top of the Theta Leaderboard once again! His eyes snapped open and his mouth hung wide in speechless shock. Finally he stammered some words out.

"How...how...how...did you do that?"

Mase's grin got even wider. "We all have our hobbies. Yours is building flight simulators. Mine is manipulating different Ship systems. The Leaderboard is managed by a low level and weak AI. I was bored one night years ago and figured out how to hack the scoring system."

Zax was dumbfounded. "Do you mean to tell me that's why you're at the top of the Zeta Leaderboard—cheating?"

Mase shook his head vehemently. "Absolutely not. I would be at the top of the Zeta Leaderboard regardless. My score is so absurdly high thanks to this little trick."

"Aren't you worried someone is going to find out? They'll put you out an airlock without blinking an eye when this gets discovered. Put my demerits back! I don't want to be mixed up with this in any way!"

"Relax, Zax, relax. I wouldn't do anything that would put either of us at risk. There are strict rules I follow. You understand how all of the Ship's AIs work, right? They all communicate with each other but are independent and discrete? That's what makes this safe. The AI that runs the Leaderboard is one of the simplest systems. It takes inputs from members of the Crew authorized to apply credits and demerits. It also listens to various systems authorized to apply automated demerits.

"Let's use the AI that monitors the showers as an example. That AI fires off a message to the Leaderboard telling it to deduct demerits when it sees someone violating the rules. The shower AI has been programmed to trust that the Leaderboard will do its job. When the shower AI receives confirmation the demerits have been applied, it forgets about the infraction. It doesn't have any need to remember the information so it doesn't. The Leaderboard is the only system that stores the data."

Mase stopped speaking and stared at him expectantly. The implications of what the boy described were clear to Zax.

"So, what you're telling me is that when you remove the Leaderboard's record of automated demerits there isn't any other record out there?"

"That's exactly right. I never touch scores from an officer or instructor punishing me. If they looked at the system later on, they might notice the missing demerits. There's no other record for automated demerits. They cease to exist once they've been erased from the Leaderboard."

Zax fell silent. If he hadn't seen the evidence with his own eyes, he never would have believed it possible. There was one more thing bothering him about all of it.

"Why are you telling me this? Aren't you worried I can get you tossed out an airlock?"

Mase shook his head once again. "Nope. I was confident you were both smart enough and ambitious enough you'd want to take advantage of this. The look on your face when you saw yourself back on top confirmed that assumption. Besides—who's going to believe you even if you did turn me in? You've already got a reputation for making up crazy stories. I can't think of one crazier than a fourteen-year-old hacking into the Ship's mighty AI."

Zax hated to admit the boy was right, but he was. Especially about that first part.

CHAPTER TWENTY-THREE

I don't see a reason to stick around here any longer.

The Boss was startled when the Flight Ops hatch opened. The prior day's scouting mission had reported the colony was empty like all the rest, so they were making their final preparations for the Transit into orbit to launch a landing party. No one should have been entering the compartment. He made eye contact with Imair as she entered and she nodded a greeting. The Boss suppressed his true feelings and reciprocated.

"Madam President—I wasn't expecting you to join us."

"Hello, Boss. I hope I'm not disturbing anything. I realized I've never been in Flight Ops while we have a surface operation exploring a colony. After our conversation yesterday, I thought today might be a good opportunity."

"By all means, ma'am. I've meant to invite you in to observe."

It was almost impossible to get the words out with a straight face, but it was important to give the team the impression he welcomed her presence rather than having it forced upon him. The Boss was pleased when no one gave it a moment's consideration. They all turned back to their workstations after the interruption with one exception. Zax continued to stare at Imair for a few extra beats until the boy noticed he was being observed. He glanced at the Boss and then turned his attention back to the threat board. Imair had also caught the cadet looking at her and she turned to the Boss and spoke.

"Boss—if I may—"

"Madam President—I'm sorry to cut you off, but the team is preparing and our rule in Flight Ops is that we don't speak aloud unless it's something critical for the entire compartment to hear. Comms—please get a subvoc for President Imair."

The Boss was surprised when Imair took the subvoc that was offered and knew to expand the device and place it over her head. He didn't realize she had worn one before and had expected he would have to explain how to use it. She contacted him on a private channel.

"Thank you, Boss. I'm sorry to have disturbed your team."

"Not a problem, Madam President. Was there something you wanted to ask?"

"Yes—may I interrupt whatever preparations Zax is making? I haven't seen the boy in a while and would like to say hello."

"That's fine, ma'am, as he's actually not critical at this moment."

A sec later Zax's face revealed Imair had contacted him on a private channel. The boy looked up from his workstation at the civilian woman. Their conversation went on for a few mins, and the Boss found himself becoming more and more curious about what they might be discussing. It struck the Boss as particularly odd that she would spend so much time conversing with the cadet when she hadn't seemed to even acknowledge one of her top lieutenants sitting right next to him. He made a mental note to check in with the boy later and see what Imair had wanted with him.

A few mins later the preparations were complete. After a status check with all workstations, the Boss gave the order to jump. He was the first in the compartment to awaken afterwards and was relieved the threat board did not reveal anything worrisome. The system and the colony were indeed empty as the scout ship had reported. Once everyone in the compartment was awake, he began issuing orders.

"Threat—stay focused and on the lookout for *anything* unusual. Scan—run a deep scan on the planet. I see there are no initial signs of human life, but

I need to be certain. Flight—don't launch the scout ship just yet but have them on a five min countdown. If we see anything that warrants a closer look, I want to be on it. Nav—I'm sending you our next destination and want a course plotted and ready to go. By the look of things, we aren't going to be sticking around here for long. I want best possible speed to our next planet."

The Boss leaned back and marveled how his team focused on their work. He glanced over at Imair and was frustrated to see the woman had pulled out a slate. If she was going disturb the team by showing up, at least she should observe their activity. After a few mins the man at the Scan workstation spoke aloud.

"Boss—I show zero signs of human life on the planet. The colony appears as empty as all of the others have been."

Everyone looked at him expectantly. A private message came in from Imair.

"Well, Boss, would you advise me to do anything different than what we've already discussed?"

The Boss wanted to advise the woman to get the hell out of his compartment, but he paused to consider a more appropriate reply. Before he could say anything, Zax spoke from across the compartment.

"Boss—I've got a bogey on the board. Initial report shows an unknown signature, but I'm analyzing further. Whatever it is, it's pretty small and very far out so shouldn't be any threat."

Great. Just great. He had wanted to send a landing party for one last chance to gather evidence about what might be going on with all of these colonies, but they would need to deal with some unknown alien first. He was about to scramble the Alert Two fighters when a private message came in from Alpha.

"Boss—we need to get out of here right now. You don't want to let the cadet finish his analysis of that bogey."

The Boss didn't appreciate the cryptic message from Alpha, but he was fairly certain he understood its deeper meaning. If he was right, he agreed with the AI's assessment. He moved to enact its advice.

"All stations—emergency jump in thirty secs."

The compartment buzzed with frantic preparations. A private message arrived from Zax.

"Sir—I'm working on identifying the bogey, and it's still far enough away that we're safe. Why are we jumping so fast?"

Zax stared at him and waited for an answer. The Boss usually reprimanded staff for asking questions rather than focusing on their jobs in the middle of an alert situation. Given Alpha's warning, he chose to keep Zax engaged and distracted instead.

"If we were still pursuing our original Mission, then we'd stick around to deal with the bogey and then make Landfall. But now? The colony is dead like all the rest. Let's not bother sticking around to see whatever alien has shown up. The President and I have already agreed on our next destination, and I

want to get moving that way sooner than later. Would you suggest doing anything different?"

Zax shook his head. *"Thank you, sir. That explanation makes perfect sense."*

The boy turned his attention back to his workstation, and the Boss chewed his cigar furiously during the remaining few secs before the Transit drove them all into unconsciousness.

CHAPTER TWENTY-FOUR

Forget it.

"I'm positive it was the same type of human spacecraft that shot Flight Ops when we patched the panorama. I think the Boss didn't want me to figure it out which is why he jumped us out of the system so quickly. I can't figure out why he's trying to hide it, but I know he is."

Zax had agonized before dinner whether he would share his suspicions with Kalare. He initially concluded yes but flipped to no when Mase showed up and sat down without being invited. Zax switched back to yes once he concluded there was zero danger in letting Mase in on the secret given his incriminating information about the young Zeta. He dropped his bombshell and waited for the reactions.

Mase glanced up briefly and raised an eyebrow but then tucked back into his meal. Kalare was in the process of raising a forkful of food to her mouth, and her eyes went wide. She paused for a moment, placed it back down, and then slowly shook her head.

"Why are you doing this, Zax? Are you trying to destroy your career again? Or maybe get yourself Culled this time? I don't understand you one bit when it comes to all of this stuff. The Boss saved the Ship and then put you into the Pilot Academy where you belong. Now you want to start digging around for insane conspiracy theories about him all over again. What's wrong with you?"

Her expression was gentle, but there was a harsh edge to Kalare's voice. Zax knew deep down he should drop the topic, but too much stress had built up for too long. It needed an outlet.

"What's wrong with me? How about we focus on what's wrong with you instead? You're supposed to be my friend, and yet every time I try to talk to you about the Boss you react like this. Why can't you help me instead of shutting me down? Or, are you too busy with your new buddy, Aleron?"

Kalare's gentle expression evaporated and was replaced with something that was predominantly anger, though tinged with sadness.

"Why can't I help you? Why do you think I am still sitting here in the first place, Zax? I've turned my life upside down in order to help you ever since you told me about Mikedo's message. Don't you remember I was going to drop out of Flight altogether and join the Marines? I pushed my own fears and feelings aside to stick around and dig up dirt about the Boss. I did that for you! Well—I spent months digging and saw nothing. That's not true. I saw lots of stuff, but it was all the exact opposite of what you were worried about. I've tried telling you this over and over again for months, and you just won't listen. I had hoped you'd come to your senses since you hadn't brought it up for a while, but I guess you've just been keeping it to yourself."

Zax opened his mouth to reply, but Kalare threw her hand in his face to cut him off.

"As for Aleron, why are you always giving me such grief about him? Have you even noticed how he's stopped bothering you these last few months? You think that just happened magically, or did it somehow cross your mind that I might have used my new relationship with him to influence his behavior? And now you're sitting here yelling at me about how I'm not helping you. Do you have any clue how much that hurts after what I've done for going on two years?"

Zax's face flushed. He knew he should retreat to let everyone's feelings calm, but didn't stop himself.

"You weren't there at the end of the Revolution, Kalare. You didn't see what he did!"

"I know! I was off in a passageway bleeding out from a gut wound and about to die! You never bothered to tell me what he did. Whenever we spoke about it, you instantly flew out of control just like you are right now!

Forget it. I don't need this anymore. I've done everything I can for you, Zax. Maybe your new buddy here can be your conspiracy assistant because I quit!"

Kalare stomped away. Mase took notice when she pushed her chair back and watched her walk out of the mess hall. When the hatch shut behind her, he turned to Zax and grinned.

"Wow."

"Shut up, Mase!"

Zax regretted yelling, but it didn't faze the Zeta in the least. He tried to pretend the boy wasn't there by staring intently at the nutripellet in his hand as he unwrapped it. Mase cleared his throat after a few min and Zax met his gaze.

"There's one thing I'm confused about."

Zax sighed but then tilted his head to signal he was listening.

"You said the bogey from today matched a human fighter the Ship encountered previously. I thought the only human spacecraft we've seen was the one found on that planet. The one in the jungle."

"That's the one the Omegas have admitted to, and it was only because I broadcast that video. There was actually another a few weeks earlier. Do you remember when we lost that tanker and bunch of fighters during a fuel harvesting operation? One of the pilots insisted before he died that the craft he saw was human, but then we were all told that Alpha analyzed the data and concluded it wasn't. I have it from a trustworthy authority that Alpha and the Omegas lied to us about that encounter."

"Interesting." Mase paused for a moment before he continued. "Why do you think today's bogey was a match?"

"My gut. There was something about the way it moved that felt familiar. I tried to convince the Boss to stick around the system long enough to identify the inbound, but he blew me off."

Mase's face remained expressionless, but his eyes lit up. He was quiet for a few secs until he abruptly stood and turned to walk away. Zax called after him.

"Hey—what are you doing? Where are you going? What did I say?"

Mase kept walking but replied over his shoulder. "I've got an idea about something. Nothing to bother you with. Yet."

CHAPTER TWENTY-FIVE

Any other questions?

"Why are you idiots so incompetent? Do you want to lose your slots on this spaceship, or are you going to figure out how to give me what I'm looking for?"

Adan glared around the room at the finest scientists and engineers the West had ever produced. Brilliant women and men who had once ruled their own institutes and labs avoided his gaze sheepishly. His blood rose again and he was about to unleash another torrent when Markev cleared his throat. Adan glanced over and his assistant gave their secret signal that let him know he needed to pause whatever he was doing and regroup. Instead of speaking, Adan stood and walked over to the massive panorama.

The view was breathtaking. Hundreds of towers thrust skyward from the asteroid—some complete but most with construction equipment scurrying around like so many insects building a hive. The scene was lit from behind by the brightness of Earth. Their current orbital position provided a spectacular view of the latest megacyclone bearing down on Oceania. All of the islands in the southern ocean had been submerged decades earlier, and the largest countries in the region had lost large swaths of their territory. Even the highest ground in those remaining areas was under threat by the approaching storm with its Category Twenty winds and ocean surge. Adan finally turned back to the group and spoke.

"You people were given two challenges—scale up the FTL so it can transport something as large as this asteroid and scale down the inertial dampeners so they can function on something as small as a tactical fighter. I'm thrilled you've made such great progress on the first item, but I'm positively dismayed you have utterly failed at the second. Fifty percent success might as well be one hundred percent failure at this critical stage of the project!"

A hand shot up in the second row of seats, and Adan acknowledged the young woman.

"Why is it so important that we adapt the dampeners for these small spacecraft? Just who do you think you're going to battle with these fighters you want us to build?"

Adan had an answer but was unable to share it. The Chancellor had placed him under penalty of death if anyone beyond an incredibly tight circle became aware of the alien spaceships a series of governments had long stored in the desert. Though most of the technology on the ships was incomprehensible, his team had managed to reverse engineer critical functionality that had long eluded the pitiful government researchers. The bottom line was that these spacecraft provided evidence of multiple alien species who explored the universe armed with advanced weaponry. Adan's spaceship needed the capacity to defend itself if it was to set off into that dangerous and unknown abyss. He didn't want to lie so instead issued a more direct response to the question.

"Get this woman a spacesuit and send her out the nearest airlock. She can try to latch on to one of the tower construction crews and beg a ride back down to Earth. If she resists, skip the spacesuit."

It was probably not the calm and collected answer that Markev envisioned when he gave the signal a moment earlier, but the bodyguard nodded at two guards. They grabbed the scientist and escorted her out of the compartment. Adan turned back to the room.

"Any other questions?" Silence. "I didn't think so. Now get out of here and get it done."

Markev stayed back and addressed his boss once the room was empty.

"She was pretty talented, sir, wasn't she?"

Adan shook his head. "She had already served her purpose with what's been accomplished around the FTL. At this stage, she was deadweight and I needed to light a fire under all of them."

"Putting aside my opinion about whether that was an effective approach or not, you're not acting like yourself, sir."

"Do you want to see the other side of an airlock hatch as well?" Adan smiled after a second to make it clear he was joking. "I know, I know. It's all of these FTL test flights. I'm piloting even more of them since you took yourself out of the rotation."

"And now that I have I'm feeling a lot better, sir. I don't know what kind of effect it's having on our minds, but I swear there's something going on besides simple exhaustion. The fact we're getting knocked unconscious without explanation each time we use the engine should be more than enough to tell you that."

Adan nodded slowly. "We're almost done with the final set of tests, and then I'll be able to take a break as well. Since you're the only person I trust as much as myself, I don't feel I have any choice right now. Am I going to let any of those jokers we were just talking to do anything that critical?"

"If you say so, sir. What do we have coming up here next? I noted your meeting request, but you didn't specify anything other than to block out the time and reserve the room."

Adan frowned. "I promise you're going to like this meeting even less than the previous one. At least you won't have to worry about me putting anyone out an airlock. Well—unless you continue mouthing off about my mental state."

Adan walked to a terminal and swiped at the screen for a moment. Suddenly the view of Earth through the giant panorama was replaced by the head and shoulders of the General Secretary. The man had been a former world-class athlete, and his shoulders were still so large and muscular they made his head look comically small perched upon them. Adan was impressed Markev managed to hold back any reaction to the man's face given what he had once suffered at his hands and those of his agents. The leader of the East raised an eyebrow when he noticed Markev's presence and then addressed Adan.

"I thought you were informed this would be a one-on-one call."

"Well, Mr. Secretary, then you can tell all of your aides who are sitting off camera they should leave. At least I have granted you the courtesy of having mine be visible."

"Does the Chancellor know we're meeting?"

Adan grinned. "Now that brings up a fun vision—the three of us around a table tossing back a few drinks and trying to talk this out together." The General Secretary remained stone-faced so Adan continued. "I have told her nothing, but I expect she knew there would be a discussion at some point. The Chancellor may be upset that I've cut her out of the negotiations, but we have an agreement that I will move as fast as I need and she will stay out of my way."

"In previous discussions she and I have had, she has made it clear we'll find an accommodation that makes all of us happy. I hope you share that attitude, Adan, or there are likely to be significant roadblocks that will appear and prevent you from finishing your little project."

Adan detested the man and everything his people believed, but he needed what they had and forced himself to choke down his distaste.

"Yes, Mr. Secretary. She made it clear you were throwing threats around. Frankly, I'd love to see you try and stop me at this point, but the time for fun and games has passed. Let's get down to business. What are you looking for?"

"Charming as always, Adan. I'm well aware you've already agreed to give the Chancellor one half of the million passenger slots you'll have on that spaceship. I'm sure you're worried I'm here to grab a large chunk of the others, but the good news is I want zero of them. What I need instead is enough space for five million of our citizens to travel in an Uploaded state. This takes a tiny fraction of the space and zero consumable resources as compared to transporting live bodies. In addition to the Uploaded, we'll also need to bring along a couple of our Skin production facilities and sufficient feedstock to generate new Skins when we ultimately get resettled on a new planet of our choosing."

It took all of Adan's willpower to not shudder when the man referred to Skins. The discovery of consciousness transferral a hundred years earlier created the schism which ultimately birthed the West and East blocs and their longstanding enmity. The people of the East were willing to toss aside their bodies in the name of reducing their ecological footprint while the West held true to the belief that saving Earth was useless if it required people to discard their physical humanity in the process. An uneasy truce was held together only through the certitude that any amount of modern warfare would tip the planet into immediate collapse. Instead of all-out conflict, a never-ending stream of low-level clashes and espionage had kept the two sides at each other's throats for generations.

Markev had battled on the front lines of those skirmishes before hiring on with Adan and still bore significant scars—both physical and mental. His assistant's glare practically burnt a hole in the side of his face, but Adan was unable to meet Markev's eyes. He focused on the General Secretary's instead which did not blink as he responded.

"That's an eminently reasonable request, Mr. Secretary. I will agree to it in exchange for my unreasonable request. This is non-negotiable, sir. A simple yes or no will suffice. You will send me your top scientists and engineers, in bodily form, to help me adapt your Upload technology for a critical need we have. What say you, sir?"

The General Secretary's eyes narrowed and he averted his eyes to someone off camera for a handful of seconds. Finally, he turned back to the camera and spoke a single word before the connection was cut and the view of Earth returned.

"Yes."

Adan exhaled. This had represented the last potential hurdle that might otherwise have proven insurmountable. Pounding footfalls approached, and Adan turned to find Markev charging like a wild bull. The giant bodyguard grabbed Adan by the elbows, pinned his arms to his sides, and lifted him a meter off the deck. The man's face burned crimson with rage.

"What in holy hell was that about? Why did you just agree to allow those creatures on our spaceship? What problem do you have which you legitimately believe is best solved with the help of a monster like that?"

Adan lowered his voice to a whisper. "I'm sorry, Markev. I'm sorry. I know how upsetting this must be for you. If you can please put me down, I'll explain."

Markev glared at him silently for nearly a minute and then dropped him to the deck. Adan rubbed at the spots where his arms had been held and envisioned the bruises which were surely forming. Finally he spoke in a calm, measured tone.

"Of course I'm aware of your personal history with the General Secretary. And you have to know I want nothing to do with him or anyone else in the East. But you also know what we're up against. You've seen the alien spacecraft that have visited Earth. If we don't have a way of protecting ourselves when we head out there, then all of this work will have been for nothing. There's one best way to do that.

"Aircraft carriers revolutionized warfare back in the twentieth century as mobile military bases that projected tremendous destructive power thousands of kilometers in all directions. We must become the spacefaring equivalent. If we don't have tactical fighters to hold off attackers well away from the asteroid, then we'll be dead the first time we encounter hostile aliens. The human body can't withstand enough g-forces to be useful when piloting at the kind of speeds we need, and you know as well as I do that we may never be able to adapt the inertial dampeners to something as small as a fighter. I've evaluated this from every angle, and the only solution I can see is to use some form of temporarily transferred consciousness to get pilots into the fighters. If there was any other way I'd take it, and I'm still hoping for a miracle with the dampeners, but I don't want to rely on a long shot. Do you understand?"

Adan stared imploringly at his bodyguard. Markev had been clenching and unclenching his fists throughout the explanation, but the man's facial expression had softened ever so slightly by the end. He paused for a few seconds once Adan was done speaking and then nodded curtly and strode out of the compartment.

Adan turned back to the panorama. Their orbit had taken them over the western hemisphere. Another megacyclone was delivering punishing ocean surges to areas which had been hundreds of kilometers inland only a century earlier. Humanity's time on Earth was nearly over—one way or another.

CHAPTER TWENTY-SIX

That sounds like a great plan, Boss.

"Ants?"

The Boss smiled at Imair before he replied. "Yes, Madam President. That's our nickname for them. It's a species of alien the Ship has encountered many times over the last thousand years or so. They bear a striking resemblance to the ants we have in our biomes, other than being about a thousand times larger."

"Interesting. Tell me about them."

The Boss took out a slate and called up an image.

"We've seen two different body types in our interactions with these aliens. The dark green and brown one on the left in this image is what we call a worker. They stand about two meters tall and are incredibly docile. You can walk right up and grab one of its three-fingered hands, and it will act as if you don't exist. It's almost like they can't see you're there, though given how their heads are entirely covered with eyeballs that seems unlikely."

The Boss gestured to the right of the image. "This green and red striped specimen is what we call a warrior. As you can guess by the name, they're anything but docile. They stand about four meters and are fierce and deadly. The only weapon we've ever seen them use is a blade like this one is holding here, but they can throw it with accuracy and killing force that rivals our blasters."

"What about their technology, Boss? Their more advanced weapons? Their spacecraft?"

"That's what's most intriguing about these bugs, ma'am. We've never seen any of it. We've encountered them hundreds of times all across the universe, but every single instance has been on a planet where there's a colony that's living a simple, agrarian existence. Other than the bladed weapons, the only tools we've ever seen are basic digging implements."

Imair was quiet for a min. The time since their scout ship returned had been a whirlwind of information she was still processing. It all started with the planet itself. True to its classification as a nine on the habitability scale, pictures of the planet took her breath away. Blue oceans of fresh, drinkable water separated two large continents and another dozen smaller ones.

The most exciting information was that preliminary scans revealed the presence of the colonists. This was tempered by the realization they had scattered into pockets on one of the continents. The colony itself was dead and deserted. Even more disconcerting was the discovery of the alien presence.

Now it was time to consider all of that information and finalize a course of action. Imair was nearly settled on what she wanted to do next but needed one final clarification.

"Does it appear that any of the ants are on the same continent as the colonists?"

"No, Madam President. This is the largest ant colony we've ever encountered, but the aliens are located exclusively on the other large continent."

"Thank you, Boss. This has been helpful. Do you have any recommendations for next steps?"

"Yes, ma'am. Our drones are completing a survey of both the colonists' continent and the ants' continent. Assuming that everything looks as expected, then we can send a mission to the surface to investigate the colony and make contact. I've advocated previously that we should not engage with any colonists, but I no longer believe that is prudent given what we've seen at all of the other colonies. We need to learn what is going on with the people we've left behind."

"That sounds like a great plan, Boss, and I agree. You went along with some of the earlier expeditions to the empty colonies, so I'm curious if you're planning to go down with this one?"

"Absolutely, ma'am."

"Excellent. Then I will join you as well."

The man paused and Imair waited in the uncomfortable silence. She no longer had a window into his thoughts after sharing her observations about his cigar-chewing giveaway one evening over drinks a couple months earlier. It was intended as a signal of trust and had seemingly landed in a positive fashion since his attitude toward her had become far more generous in the time since. The chewed, ragged tip of the Boss's cigar peeked out from the pocket of his shirt. It glistened with saliva which bore witness to how he had only recently removed it from his mouth. Clearly, he had taken the feedback and modified his behavior accordingly. Finally, he spoke.

"With all due respect, ma'am, I think that's an incredibly bad idea. Even after extensive drone surveys, we never know what kind of danger we might run into down on the surface of a planet."

Imair stared at the man intently for a few secs before challenging him. "I'm sorry, Boss, but I'm confused. This planet was extensively surveyed prior to the colony being established, so we're already highly knowledgeable about its flora and fauna. Yes—there are now aliens present, but you just explained to me that we've encountered these aliens hundreds of times across a thousand years, so we are well familiar with them. The aliens are exclusively located across a giant ocean, and we are certain they have no technology or other means to cross it. The biggest unknowns in the equation are the colonists themselves, right?"

The Boss retained a stoic expression, but he nodded his head and Imair continued.

"So, are you telling me it will be too difficult for a group of Marines to keep me safe from a bunch of colonists who were not left any weapons more powerful than stunstiks? Who appear to have abandoned their colony and all of its technology to live a primitive life in the jungle?"

"Ma'am—the people I'm bringing down are all trained Crew. The Marines are experts, and even the Flight team are all sufficiently competent to handle any surprise we might encounter. Bringing along a civilian, even someone I know to be as capable as you, strikes me as a bad idea. Besides—isn't it important that you remain up here to continue to inspire the civilian population?"

"OK, Boss, that last bit wasn't funny at all. I'm fully aware I might be safer strolling naked through that ant colony than walking through parts of the Ship right now. Our civilians are getting restless, and I'm sure you've heard how violent things have become in some of their sectors. They need a positive message to help maintain their hope. The best way I can deliver a message like that is if I see whatever is happening down there first hand. If I can touch and smell a planet that is even more beautiful than Earth, it will help me motivate the civilians to stay hopeful and excited about this journey. Do you understand?"

"I understand, Madam President, but my reservations remain. I'll support your decision and do everything necessary to keep you safe down there."

"Thanks, Boss. One last thing. I need Rege to come with us too."

A look of absolute distaste crossed the Boss's face, but he quickly recovered and nodded. "By all means, ma'am." He turned and left.

Imair understood why the Boss didn't want anything to do with Rege. Truth be told, she didn't either. She had become more and more convinced he was a prime source of the agitation that was roiling the civilian sectors, however, and she refused to leave him on the Ship unsupervised. He'd either come around to supporting the message she wanted to deliver after visiting the planet or perhaps he wouldn't return from it.

CHAPTER TWENTY-SEVEN

You got to wear ChamWare?

Thrilled he would get to keep it down for the first time in eleven months, Zax savored a bite from one of his favorite pastries. The non-stop pace of daily Transits had prevented him from eating real breakfast other than a couple of times when he broke down and did so in spite of the knowledge he would toss the meal a few hours later. With no Transit scheduled, Zax loaded up his tray and then sat at his usual table.

The prospect of actual food was exciting, but Zax's heart ached at the memories it triggered of raucous meals where he sat with Kalare and listened to her nonstop stories. Unfortunately, their interactions since the last colony visit had been infrequent and generally unpleasant. Zax had hoped a rapprochement was in the offing when they met for breakfast to celebrate Kalare's graduation from the Pilot Academy and both of their advancement from Theta into Kappa Cadre, but the meal swiftly turned into a disaster. It started when the Boss somehow chose that morning to visit the Crew mess for the first time in months. After the Omega stopped by their table, Kalare started to grill Zax about his feelings for the man. It was a test he failed, and she stormed off hollering how she wouldn't stand by and suffer again if Zax was determined to throw his career away.

As had become the new pattern, Mase sat across from him in Kalare's old seat. Zax was grateful to have Mase to sit with, even with the boy being less conversational than he was. There were many days where an entire meal went by without any words uttered between them other than quick greetings and farewells. The boy's outward demeanor was different than usual, so Zax asked if anything was wrong.

"I'm nervous about this trip down to the planet. I've got a weird feeling in the pit of my stomach."

"I understand, Mase. I was a wreck the first time I left the Ship. Is there anything in particular you're worried about?"

"I don't know how I'm going to handle all the open space. I experienced massive vertigo in the simulator whenever we did surface-based exercises. All of that empty space messes with my head. You'd think I would have the same problem when I'm flying. I suppose it's feeling a complete lack of control when I'm walking on the surface. I know I can handle anything that happens when I'm on stick in a fighter."

Zax smiled at the boy. "You kicked butt on that last surface simulation we did, so I'm sure you're going to do fine. Besides—there really isn't much you have to worry about. Help Kalare drive the bus, and then let the Marines do their thing. They aren't going to let you get into any trouble. As long as you listen to them, at least."

"Thanks, Zax. Does it bother you that I'm flying down with Kalare?"

"No." Zax was lying and they both knew it. "I'm sure it's only because I'm Maverick, and Major Eryn wants to keep the best co-pilot to make things easier for herself."

"Ha, ha. You're funny. What have you heard about the planet?"

"Probably not much more than you. It was great to hear gravity is only 90 percent of what we're used to on the Ship and the oxygen levels are almost a perfect match. The last time I traveled to a planet, it had more gravity and less oxygen and that made things way more challenging. I also had to wear ChamWare which I'd just as soon avoid for the rest of my life." Zax shuddered at the visceral memory of overheated claustrophobia.

Mase's mouth opened wide. "You got to wear ChamWare? Cool! We've never talked about that trip. What was it like?"

Zax really wasn't in the mood to relive one of his most painful memories, but he owed it to Mase to share at least a little. His ranking atop the Leaderboard had never been better thanks to the boy's ability to go in and clean out all of the silly automated demerits that previously had dragged him down. Sometimes Zax experienced a twinge of guilt about allowing Mase to work his magic, but then some Omega would hit him with an unfair slug of demerits and he would rationalize that it all evened out in the end. He dove into the story.

"It was a couple of years ago. The Boss set up a competition between me and Kalare to determine who he was going to mentor. He ran us through crazy training with the Marines and this Flight officer named Mikedo to see how we would each perform under intense pressure. This all happened at the same time we were preparing to make Landfall, so the last part of the training was a trip down to the surface to help evaluate a potential colony."

Emotions started to well up as Zax recalled all of those events. For the first time ever, the sadness did not revolve around memories of Mikedo. Instead, Zax found himself mourning the loss of his friendship with Kalare. He was so often frustrated by her quirks when they first met, but, over the course of that training and what came afterwards, he grew quite fond of her. He missed her something fierce but pushed those feelings aside so he wouldn't have to discuss them with Mase. He continued.

"That planet had ants too, so we wore ChamWare and scouted out their settlement. We didn't think there were any warriors present and it was supposed to be a low risk mission, but then one of the Marines I was with got attacked. The thing I remember most about the planet was the trees. They were impossibly tall, and even better, they were carnivorous. If you brushed up against one, it would grab you and eat you whole."

Mase appeared impressed. "That's so cool! Wait—wasn't that the same planet where we discovered the human fighter?"

"Yeah." Zax paused for another deep breath. "It was the officer I mentioned earlier, Mikedo, who captured that famous video and eventually sent it to me. I think you know the rest of the story."

Mase whistled in appreciation. "Holy crap, Zax. I never understood how you were the one who got your hands on that video. It all makes more sense, now. Why did she send it to you? What made you expose it the way you did?"

Zax didn't want to think about the whole episode any further. A giant, swirling mass of emotion roiled the breakfast in his belly that he so desperately wanted to keep. He didn't want to lie to the boy, but he didn't feel they were close enough yet to share even a hint of the truth. He deflected the questions instead.

"Let's talk about this some other day. We've got to get to the briefing. If there's one thing you need to learn about the Marines, it's they have a crazy obsession about never being late."

"Hey—you can't stop right at the good part like that!" The boy appeared disappointed, but he stood up and gathered his trash regardless. "I'm not going to share with you my exciting news since you won't finish your story. It has to do with the humans as well. You're going to be disappointed when you learn that you missed a chance to hear it sooner."

Zax couldn't care less about whatever nonsense the boy was spouting at that moment. He needed an escape. "My stomach's not feeling well. You better go ahead. I'll meet you at the briefing."

Mase waved goodbye and Zax walked toward the head. He didn't really need the bathroom, so instead he leaned against the bulkhead next to it for a few mins. His emotions finally settled and eventually his stomach did as well. He checked the time and bolted at double-time pace. He didn't want to suffer the indignity of being late to a briefing with a room full of Marines.

CHAPTER TWENTY-EIGHT

Sounds about right for civilians.

Zax was winded but made it to the briefing room with twenty-seven secs to spare. It was the same compartment where he had his last planet briefing, though the room was far more crowded this time. Imair sat in the front row with the Flight Boss on one side and Sergeant Bailee on the other. Mase sat behind them, and Zax studiously avoided eye contact with the boy. He was heading toward the back of the compartment when he noticed Kalare and Aleron sitting together in the last row. He detoured quickly and grabbed a seat in the middle of the room.

Major Odon stood ramrod straight in front of everyone. The stern Marine, who led their premier recon unit Charlie Company, remained as imposing as when Zax had first encountered him at a similar briefing two years earlier. A vivid flashback to seeing the Marine through a drug-induced haze made Zax shiver. The major appeared more fearsome than usual since he was standing next to Lieutenant Nineem. The Flight officer from the exobiology unit was even softer and doughier than he had been when he delivered that previous briefing. Odon started to speak the instant the meeting was scheduled to start.

"Charlie Company—we're *incredibly fortunate* to be joined on this recon by a large contingent from Flight. We'll also have a couple of civilians along as guests. President Imair and another member of her staff—"

It was impossible for Rege to have timed his entrance any better. Or, based on Major Odon's facial expression, any worse. The Marine charged at the civilian as he walked through the hatch and got right up into his face with a fusillade of angry questions.

"What is your malfunction, civilian? Were you not told when this briefing would start? Do they not teach you civilians how to tell time?"

A woman's voice boomed through the compartment.

"Stand down, Major."

Odon spun around and glared at Imair. He turned slightly to check in with the Flight Boss and she spoke again.

"There's no need to look at him, Marine. I'm in charge here. Understood?"

The major glared at Imair for another couple of secs before he replied. "Understood, *Madam President.*"

Incredibly, Rege pressed his luck further and bumped up against the furious Marine's shoulder as he moved past him to take a seat. The major tensed as if he was contemplating ripping the civilian to shreds. The Flight Boss cleared his throat and broke the spell. The Marine stormed to the back of the compartment with barely contained rage emanating off him.

All eyes turned to Lieutenant Nineem, who appeared relieved that someone else had distracted Odon from his own existence. He dimmed the lights and brought up a holoimage of the planet. It was even more beautiful than the pictures of ancient Earth, and Zax was mesmerized.

"Approximately 1,500 years have elapsed on this planet since we established its colony. Based on our initial drone surveys, it does not appear that very much has changed since then. All of the water on the planet is potable. Its surface is covered with wild fruit and vegetable plants which are all safe to eat from as long as you stay away from anything purple in color. It also teems with miniature grazing animals which I've been told are both delicious and nutritious. The apex predators are equally small and therefore pose nothing but a minor annoyance to anything as large as a human.

"With 90 percent of standard gravity and ideal oxygen levels, this planet is nearly an optimal target for human settlement. The only measure by which it lacks when evaluated on the human habitability scale is that the ratio of landmass to water is only half of Earth's. It would nonetheless make an amazing homeworld, albeit one that is more limited than Earth with regards to the population it can support."

The lieutenant switched the image to display a group of the alien ants. "One change we've identified since the colony was first established is the presence of our friends the ants. The good news is the aliens are exclusively located on one of the two largest continents with no sign they have ever been present on any of the other landmasses—most importantly the other large continent where our colonists are located. Since we know the ants don't have any technology beyond simple tools, we can guarantee you won't encounter any of them while you explore the colony and track down the colonists."

The ants disappeared and were replaced with an image of the colonists. There were audible gasps around the room at the sight of humans who wore nothing but patched together animal skins. Nineem grinned.

"Yeah—it's a pretty grisly sight. The images remind me of pictures I've seen from ancient Earth of the earliest, barely sentient homo sapiens—what they called the cavemen."

One of the Marines muttered under his breath, but loudly enough to be heard around the compartment, "Seems about right for civilians."

There were multiple sniggers and Nineem paused uncomfortably. The Boss shot out of his chair.

"I don't want to hear another word like that, Marines. The next person who disrespects President Imair is going out an airlock!"

The Omega continued to glare in the direction the comment had come from until Imair reached up and rested her hand on his elbow. He sat down and Nineem continued.

"The colonists have broken up into dozens of isolated groups which are scattered around the continent. This image is taken from the group that is closest to the physical remains of the colony. There does not appear to be any signs of violence or destruction, and we have no ideas as to why the colony was abandoned. We also have limited guesses as to the current status of their civilization. My team suggests you approach the colonists with great care and assume they are dangerous and unpredictable primates until you are able to prove otherwise. Any questions?"

There were none, so Major Odon stood and spoke from his position at the back of the room. "Marines—pack out a full battle load. We aren't going to deploy in ChamWare, but I want us to have it so we're prepared for anything. Flight personnel and civilians should report to the Marine armory for a full kit which will include your own ChamWare. We take off at 0700 and," he glared at Rege, "the bus waits for no one."

Zax stood and made to leave until his name was called above the tumult of the dispersing group. Major Eryn gestured him toward her and he approached.

"Hello, Zax. Do you have any questions or concerns about our flight tomorrow?"

"No, ma'am. Thank you for asking. I was surprised I got invited along."

"I'll be honest and say it wasn't my idea. The Boss insisted on bringing you. We rarely let cadets participate in missions like this one, but I suppose the Boss has no problem doing things differently to support the cadets he's mentoring."

Zax wanted to guffaw at the major's comment having learned from Mase how much the woman was doing to support him, but he managed to keep a neutral expression. She continued.

"Don't get me wrong. If I had to have any cadet participate you are certainly one of the top two I would choose. I'm sure it's no secret that I'm mentoring Mase, so you might worry that I'm not happy about how close the competition has remained between the two of you. Actually, my feelings are pretty strong in the opposite direction. We all get better when we are pushed to do so, and you and Mase are doing a fantastic job of driving each other harder and harder to get even better than you would be on your own. Just look at your Leaderboard score—you've significantly widened your lead over your nearest competition during the past year, and I have to think that has been in large part due to Mase's influence."

If she only knew. Zax smiled. "Certainly, ma'am."

"Well, if anything comes up that you're unsure of or want to check in about, please reach out to me. We'll be flying the command shuttle with the Boss aboard, and I want to be certain everything goes as smoothly as possible."

Zax turned to leave until the major made him pause with one final exhortation.

"And make sure you get a lot of rest tonight, Zax. Missions like this almost always go differently than planned, so we need to be ready for anything."

CHAPTER TWENTY-NINE

Wow.

"**S**huttle 5436—you're cleared for departure."
      The most momentous day of Zax's life had begun with a trip to the surface of a planet as a passenger on board Shuttle 5436. Two years later, he sat in the right-hand pilot seat of its flight deck. Major Eryn sat to Zax's left while the Boss, Sergeant Bailee, and Imair were arrayed directly behind them. Major Eryn had told him during preflight she wanted him to do the flying unless there was an emergency, so he replied to the controller in Flight Ops.

      "Shuttle 5436 is a go."

      Zax performed one last visual check around his craft before initiating takeoff. His nerves got the better of him, and he applied a little too much throttle. The shuttle lifted off the deck with a sudden jerk, and

Imair's hand grabbed hold of Zax's shoulder. He wasn't sure whether it was a grip of encouragement or the civilian just trying to catch her balance, but he shocked himself by leaning toward the former.

Imair had been in Zax's thoughts a lot ever since she spoke with him privately back in Flight Ops—the day they started their journey to the planet spinning beneath them. Before the unknown bogey showed up and sent them fleeing that system, she had shared a funny story about Nolly. Imair also opened up about the tremendous grief she carried knowing the boy was sacrificed as part of her Revolution.

Her expressions of remorse were thoroughly unexpected at the time, but they came across as being genuine. Zax had accepted them as an olive branch from the woman he had come to respect during a year of working together in Waste Systems. He subsequently spent many hours trying to filter the woman's actions through a different lens of who she might actually be deep down inside. By all rights the Revolution should have left the Crew in a far worse position than what Imair had created. Zax found himself fighting against his inbred bias and tipping toward the conclusion that perhaps she was not a monster after all.

They departed the hangar without further incident, and Kalare's shuttle received its clearance and followed. The shuttles flew around the Ship until their destination came into full view. The planet was similar to all of the pictures Zax had seen of Earth, with the most notable exception being the oceans were a few shades lighter blue. The two largest continents were in view and both were sprinkled with fine, wispy cloud cover. Reports had shown it was perfect weather for a flight to the surface. Imair broke the silence.

"Boss—I understand our plan was to go straight to our colony. Would it be possible for us to fly over the alien colony first instead? I'm interested in seeing it with my own eyes."

"By all means, ma'am. Cadet—instruct the other shuttle to proceed straight to the landing zone. We'll detour and then meet up with them."

"Yes, sir."

Zax replied to the Boss and then opened a private channel to connect with Kalare. He had devised a plan to use this shared adventure to initiate a thawing of their relationship, and this would be the first salvo.

"Hey, Kalare—has Mase screwed anything up yet?"

"What do you need, Shuttle 5436?"

"Come on, Kalare, why are you still acting like this? Can't we try to get back to how things were between us?"

"I repeat, what do you need, Shuttle 5436?"

This was not going as hoped, so Zax gave up in favor of waiting for a face-to-face discussion. *"We have a change in plans, and the Boss asked me to inform you. Our shuttle is going to do a flyover of the ant colony to let Imair see it up close. He wants you to proceed directly to the landing zone."*

"Acknowledged."

Kalare cut the connection after responding. Zax clearly had his work cut out for him with regards to bridging the rift between them. Her shuttle peeled away toward the continent with the human colony while he vectored his toward the one with the ants.

A few mins later their view was obscured by the superheated plasma their craft generated as it ripped through the atmosphere. When their fiery entry ended, the continent with the ant colony dominated their view. Zax turned to the Boss.

"Sir—how low should I go?"

"Let's give the President a good show, cadet. Two hundred meters."

"Yes, sir."

As they came in lower and lower, the alien colony was at first only a dark splotch against the lighter vegetation. As they got closer, the splotch began to undulate as if it was a living organism. The comparison was perfectly apt because what had previously appeared to be a solid mass resolved instead into a tremendous swarm of the ant-like creatures. They were too numerous to count, but Zax estimated it might be more than a million.

Zax chanced a glance around him to see how the other folks were reacting. Major Eryn gawked at the scene in front of them. Imair similarly stared down at the aliens with her mouth agape. Bailee, typically stone-faced, wore an expression which hinted at shock. The Boss sported a tight grin as he took in the scene and nodded in appreciation. The Omega broke the silence with a low whistle before he spoke.

"We've seen these bugs a bunch through the years but never anything quite like this. I'm impressed."

Impressed was far too much of an understatement to describe what Zax was feeling. He had never seen so many living organisms in such a small area, and he held his breath in awe. Zax contemplated the patterns of movement and was fascinated as pockets of the swarm moved in lockstep with each other. Tens of thousands of ants would form into a group that would move in unison through the swirling mass of the other creatures. What appeared at first to be a maelstrom of random movement was actually an amazing vision of large-scale coordination and choreography. Zax was mesmerized until something in the pattern caught his attention.

"Sir—the workers don't care about our presence, but I'm certain the warriors are paying attention to us."

"It's not only when we are down on the ground that their behavior toward us is different between the two types of ants. Warriors have been reported to acknowledge the presence of our shuttles and—"

Zax interrupted the Boss with a shouted warning. "One of those warriors just threw a blade at us!"

The Omega smiled. "As I was saying, warriors have even been known to throw their blades at our shuttles. I had you drop us down to two hundred meters because I knew that was out of their range. If we were going to actually land anywhere near here, we would have mapped a route that wouldn't have gotten them all riled up. Given the size of that swarm, we aren't going to visit here anytime soon. Get us over to the other continent, Zax. It's time for all of us to see our colony with our own eyes."

CHAPTER THIRTY

I agree you shouldn't trust me.

With no aliens to worry about, Zax banked the shuttle slowly around the human colony at an altitude of fifty meters. From the air, everything appeared as if the colonists had simply walked away. The drone surveys had suggested the same was true on the ground, and Zax was excited to get out and check for himself. He deftly landed the shuttle and was starting his post-flight checklist when the Boss paused before following Bailee and Imair out of the flight deck.

"Major Eryn—it was a pleasure to witness another example of the fine training you're providing at the Academy. Between Kalare and Zax, it's been fantastic to see up close how you're developing the next generation of likely Omegas. We'll talk soon about finding a bigger role where you can have an even wider impact."

The Boss left. Major Eryn smiled at him from the opposite seat.

"Well done, cadet. Well done. I'll take care of post-flight. You should go get ready. You and Kalare will accompany the Boss while Mase and I remain with the shuttles."

The major's tone was so shockingly warm that Zax feared he was blushing. "Thank you, ma'am."

Zax was walking through the shuttle to grab his kit bag when his name was called. His heart sank when he turned and discovered Aleron.

"Hey, Zax. Great job flying."

Aleron stared at him expectantly, and Zax was so taken aback that he answered automatically.

"Thank you."

"I'm glad I ran into you. I know it's a crazy time right now for what I'm going to say, but I've been trying to catch a moment alone with you and it almost feels like you've been actively avoiding me. Kalare will kill me if she knows I talked with you about this, but I'm going to trust you to do whatever you feel is best with that knowledge. I realize you don't have any reason to believe anything that comes out of my mouth, but I need you to put that aside right now and hear me out."

Zax shrugged noncommittally and Aleron continued.

"She hasn't told me what drove you two apart, but she's talked about the result a lot. She's torn up. She doesn't know how things can be fixed, but she wants to figure it out more than anything."

"Huh? She sure isn't acting that way. I keep extending peace gestures, and she shoots them down instantly."

"I know, Zax. I know. She's confused. She cares about you an awful lot, but she says you guys have some huge differences." Aleron paused before adding the rest. "I'm guessing that one of those might have to do with how she's become friends with me. If that's true, and if me pushing her away would help the situation between you two, just say the word."

Zax was momentarily speechless. "What's going on here? Have I fallen through a black hole and entered some strange dimension where you're an actual human being?"

"Yep—I deserve that. I agree you shouldn't trust me. And yet—here I stand asking you to trust me."

"Why?"

"Simple—because I owe you both. I finally managed to track down those officers who the Boss sent off during the Revolution. They're dead. I would be too if I had gone with them, and you two are the reason I didn't. I know you don't think I'm all that bright, but I'm smart enough to recognize the debt I owe."

"Cadet Zax—why are you making us wait for you?"

Sergeant Bailee's voice boomed through the empty shuttle. While Zax turned to acknowledge the man, Aleron walked away in the opposite direction without another word. Zax was stunned by such a generous offer from his lifelong foe, but he didn't have time to consider it any further with the Marine barking at him. He sprinted to where his kit bag lay and lifted it up off the deck with both hands. His growth over the last two years meant its weight didn't nearly tip him over this time around, but it was still crazy heavy. He ran to where Bailee stood tapping his foot.

"My apologies, Sergeant."

"That's the best you can do when we're almost twenty secs past our planned departure time because of you?"

There might have been a glimmer of humor in the man's eyes, but it was gone in a flash if it ever really existed. Zax cranked up his pace and ran out of the shuttle to where the rest of the landing party had assembled. The Crew from Flight were off to one side quietly talking amongst themselves. The Marines of Charlie Company were arrayed by platoon around the landing pad. They bristled with a fearsome energy and were clearly prepared for their mission—whatever it might bring.

The Boss pitched his voice loud enough to silence everyone.

"Today, for the first time in the Ship's history, we will make contact with the descendants of our colonists. We don't know what this experience is going to be like for them given we are many generations removed from anyone who knew the Ship first hand. I want you to remember the briefing and treat the colonists with caution, but don't lose sight of the fact we're about to encounter human beings. Whatever happens, I want you to exercise the utmost care and only harm any of the colonists if they represent an immediate and significant threat. Major—"

"Thank you, sir." Major Odon turned to his Marines. "I want Second Platoon to evaluate the southern half of the colony and Third Platoon to check the northern half. First Platoon will stay with me and our VIPs as we head into the main administration area. Stay sharp, Marines!"

"Sir, yes, sir!" thundered Charlie Company.

The platoons dispersed as directed, and Zax fell into step behind Sergeant Bailee. The Boss walked near the front of the formation with Imair on his left and Kalare on his right. They were surrounded, albeit unobtrusively, by a protective detail commanded by Bailee. Zax assumed this group included Marines hidden in ChamWare, though he had not yet seen any indications they were more than a rumor.

Zax tried to appreciate the beauty around him. Unlike his last sortie on a planet, Zax walked unencumbered by the sealed, sterile experience of ChamWare. There were also no man-eating trees to worry about this time around. Only a beautiful, near-perfect planet with abundance as far as the eye could see. He basked in the sweet smell of ripe fruit on the gentle breeze, the call of the animals from the trees, and the warmth of the sun on his face. He was legitimately tempted to run away from all of his frustrations back on the Ship and disappear into the jungle never to be seen again. Zax's reverie was interrupted when the Boss called for a halt in front of the colony's central building.

"Major Odon—send in a team to evaluate the administration building. It's probably going to be the same as every other abandoned colony we've visited. I'd just as soon spend as much time as I can outside."

Odon nodded and with a flurry of hand signals dispatched a squad of Marines along with a team from Engineering into the building. Zax was relieved to remain outside as he had zero interest in exploring a creepy, empty building. He breathed deep and spied from a distance as Kalare appeared to do the same. She caught his eye for a moment and then pointedly turned away. Zax considered approaching but ultimately held off to see if a better opportunity presented itself. A few mins later the group returned and reported there was nothing of interest inside the building. The Boss nodded and then spoke to the larger group once more.

"We've heard from the other platoons, and the entire colony is as boring as this building. It's time to head into the jungle and find the colonists. We know they're in there somewhere even though something about this vegetation is preventing our sensors from getting a precise lock on their position. Be ready for anything!"

The group plunged into the dense jungle. The darkness created by the thick canopy descended like a massive weight and threatened to suffocate Zax. As they moved deeper and deeper into the trees, the sounds of animals became more and more sporadic until finally they were surrounded by eerie silence.

Crack!

The snapping branch was off to Zax's left. He concluded it must belong to a Marine in ChamWare since he spun his head instantly and found nothing. He stopped and listened.

Lub-DUB, Lub-DUB.

Lub-DUB, Lub-DUB.

Lub-DUB, Lub-DUB.

Zax's heart pounded in his ears so loudly it threatened to render him otherwise deaf. His eyes had finally adjusted to the gloom, but the lack of light bathed his surroundings in monochromatic uniformity. The jungle was so thick it almost obscured the other people who were nearby. Until—movement off to the side!

THWACK!

A female voice screamed in pain. The jungle lit up with blaster fire. Zax ducked behind a tree, and a couple secs later the Major called a halt to the fire.

"What is it? Who has eyes on a target?"

No one spoke. Once again, the jungle was flooded with silence.

Zax peeked around the tree. He was about to step out when he saw them. Eyes! They were clearly human and yet somehow wildly foreign. They stared out from the face of a boy who was the same size as Zax.

The boy was almost entirely camouflaged against the jungle backdrop, and it was only the darting back and forth of his eyes which had betrayed his position. He held a blade in one hand and some form of stringed weapon in his other. Zax froze and pinged Bailee on his Plug.

"Sergeant—there's a human boy almost directly at your six. He's facing away from you toward me. Next to the tree with the notch three meters off the ground."

On the other side of the boy, Bailee turned and looked toward Zax. He continued to watch, and Zax assumed the man was communicating with someone via his Plug. Five secs later there was a rush of noise and the boy had been disarmed and was floating upside down with his head half a meter above the ground. He struggled furiously for a few secs until his head suddenly snapped back and he was knocked unconscious. A disembodied head materialized as a Marine raised the visor on his ChamWare.

"I've got him, Sergeant."

Zax was trying to fully process the sight when the Boss cried out.

"I need a medic—the President is down!"

CHAPTER THIRTY-ONE

She's practically gone!

"Kalare—come here now! I need another pair of hands!"

She had already been on the move when the Boss called for a medic, but the tone of his voice made Kalare sprint the last ten meters to his position. Imair lay on the ground, sprawled on her side. Even in the gloom of the jungle, it was clear the civilian was in extreme pain. She had been impaled by a wooden shaft that was carved to a point on one end and had colorful feathers affixed to the other. The sharp end dripped blood after entering a few centimeters to the side of Imair's navel and exiting her back at an angle. The Boss had removed his shirt and used part of it as a compress to stanch the bleeding of the exit wound. He hollered at Kalare as she approached.

"Grab that other part of my shirt and compress it around the entrance wound! She's bleeding heavily in the back, and we need to keep as much blood in her as we can."

Kalare did as instructed. There was nowhere near as much bleeding from the entrance wound as there was from the exit, but the shirt was quickly soaked through nonetheless. The Boss called out again.

"Where's my medic?"

Bailee showed up and evaluated the scene in silence before addressing the Boss.

"Sir—we've captured the shooter. It was a young boy. He's unconscious right now but can be revived whenever you're ready to interrogate him."

"Where's the medic? She's going to bleed out!"

Imair continued to writhe in pain, but the Boss's words caught her attention. She opened her eyes and looked up at Kalare.

"Is it really that bad, cadet?"

Kalare smiled at the civilian. "Ma'am—we'll get you patched up quick and you'll be as good as new." She didn't think it was a true statement based on the amount of blood seeping onto the ground, but she wanted to help calm the woman. A min later there was less blood coming out of the entrance wound, though Kalare didn't know if the change was due to the pressure she had applied or to the fact that Imair didn't have much more blood left to lose. It was more likely the latter given how the woman had stopped her struggle against the pain and descended into unconsciousness.

A Marine medic finally arrived. She approached nonchalantly and tapped the Boss on the shoulder. The Omega looked up at her and yelled.

"Where the hell have you been, Corporal?"

"My apologies, sir. One of my squadmates twisted an ankle diving for cover when the shooting started. I assumed the civilian should wait while I took care of him first."

Kalare had been around the Boss enough to recognize the man was enraged by the Marine's response, but he moved aside to allow the woman to evaluate the situation. She put her pack on the ground next to Imair and removed a medkit. It was identical to the ones back on the Ship except for being shrunk down so as to be portable. The medic extracted the diagnostic wand from the device and waved it over Imair's body starting at the exit wound on her back and moving around to the entrance wound on her belly.

Red symbols flashed on the display which Kalare understood to mean the civilian was in dire condition, and yet the Marine moved without urgency. The corporal configured the medkit by attaching two identical rectangular devices to it via transparent hoses which plugged into identical ports. The Boss appeared to become more and more agitated by the medic's slow and deliberate movements. The Marine eventually turned to the Omega.

"Sir—she has a punctured kidney. I have to remove the shaft before we can stop the bleeding. I need you and the cadet to hold her down. She's out cold now, but as soon as I start pulling this thing out, she's likely to wake up screaming."

The Boss nodded in agreement. He gestured for Kalare to hold the civilian's legs, and he pinned down her torso and arms. The medic counted down.

"Three—two—one—now!"

As expected, Imair's eyes went wide and she struggled furiously when the medic pulled the shaft out of her body. It took all of Kalare's strength to keep the woman's legs on the ground. The entrance and exit wounds, which had previously slowed to a seep, once again spewed copious blood. The medic placed her face in front of Imair's and spoke with a sharp tone.

"You need to stop moving! You're making the bleeding worse, and I won't be able to stop it!"

The Marine's words got Imair's attention and she stopped struggling, though her legs continued to shake under Kalare's grip. The civilian's eyes, which a moment earlier had gone wide in terror and pain, started to dull. An alarm bleated on the medkit, and the Boss glared at the medic.

"Get moving, Marine! She's practically gone!"

The corporal placed one of the rectangular devices against the entrance wound, and it formed a seal. She repeated the process around the exit wound with the other device and then initiated treatment. Instead of the green liquid that Kalare remembered being used to treat the Boss during the Revolution, the tubes filled with a bright yellow solution. It must have included some form of anesthetic because Imair's legs instantly stopped shaking. Kalare relaxed, and the medic signaled for her to release her hold. There were now a few more people around the scene. Major Odon stood next to Bailee, and Rege stood off to the side behind them. The male civilian observed the scene intently, though his expression was impenetrable.

The Boss released his hold on Imair and rose from the ground. He took the clean shirt Bailee held out to him and spoke once he put it on.

"Major—I need you to supervise the remaining treatment. I will hold you personally responsible if the President doesn't survive. Bailee—let's go find out why this boy decided he needed to shoot at us without asking any questions first. Kalare—come with me. There's no sense in you hanging around here any longer since the Marines *finally* have the situation under control."

Kalare followed the Boss and Bailee into the jungle back the way they came, and a min later they encountered a bizarre scene. A Marine in ChamWare had removed his visor but otherwise remained invisible. His face hung all by itself in the air two meters above a boy who was slumped unconscious on the ground. Zax was off to the side, leaning against a tree. He caught Kalare's eye with a tentative smile, but she turned away without acknowledgement.

Deep down Kalare wanted to let things get back to normal with Zax, but she found herself keeping him at arm's length. Their final argument was fairly innocuous in hindsight, but it was the culmination of a long line of disagreements about the Boss and conspiracies involving the man which Zax imagined were hidden around every corner. Kalare's experience with the Omega had been nothing but positive in all the time she had dealt with him. Her feelings about the man's character were only strengthened by what she had just witnessed. The Boss had just fought to save a woman he otherwise should have wished dead. Zax refused to listen to any reasoning that might conclude the man was innocent, and Kalare found it exhausting.

She didn't want to sit back and watch Zax throw his career away again, but that was the most likely outcome given his behavior. If Kalare was unable to save him from himself, then why should she risk the immense pain of being up close while he self-destructed a second time? Even with all of that clear in her mind, she still didn't want to give up on him. Not without at least one more run at trying to get his head right. Maybe a better outcome was possible if Kalare focused more on how her frustration wasn't about defending the Boss but rather about wanting to protect Zax. He just might listen to that. She had to try and resolved to do so soon.

The Boss and Bailee approached the young colonist. The sergeant hefted the unconscious form and held the boy upright with his arms pinned behind his back. The Boss reached out with the knuckles of his right hand and dug them vigorously into the boy's sternum. The pain forced the colonist to stir and then struggle, but his strength was no match for the Marine who restrained him. The Omega stood back and allowed the boy to shake off his disorientation.

He wore animal skins and had painted his skin to blend into the jungle, but otherwise the young colonist looked just like any other boy. That assessment changed when he finally opened his eyes. They contained dark brown irises so huge they barely left room for any white within the sockets. Dominating each iris was an equally massive, inky-black pupil. Kalare assumed it was all a genetic adaptation to living in such dense and dark jungle, and it signaled how the colonists must have abandoned their more traditional living arrangements many generations ago.

If the Boss was as shocked by the appearance of the boy's eyes as Kalare, he didn't show it. He stared intently at the boy and gave him a warm smile once it was clear the young colonist had regained full consciousness.

"Hello. Do you understand what I'm saying?"

The boy was trying to impart a sense of defiance, but his fear was obvious. "Why wouldn't I understand you? Do I look stupid or something?"

The Boss chuckled. "No, I don't think you look stupid. I do wonder if you're confused, though. Why would you start shooting at us without even trying to talk to us first?"

"You are not us. You are other."

"Other? What do you mean, other?"

"Not us. Other. We have to protect us and keep away other."

The Boss raised an eyebrow. "I understand. I'm sorry we hurt you, but we had to protect ourselves when you shot at us. Can we try to put all of that behind us and be friends?"

The boy glared at the Boss and repeated his earlier words. "Not us."

The Boss kept his disposition friendly and allowed his smile to become even wider and more welcoming. "I understand, son. You know what you know. Maybe I can talk some sense into your leaders. I want you to bring me back to your group, OK?"

The boy shook his head vehemently. "No. Not us. Keep us safe."

The Boss slowly shook his head. "I'm sorry, but I really must insist."

The boy continued to stare defiantly at the Boss. Kalare held her breath at what might come next. She didn't believe the Omega had it in him to harm someone so young, but she knew the Boss would be intent on forcing the boy to provide a location for his fellow colonists. The Omega gestured for the Marine in ChamWare to approach. The boy had been so focused on the Boss right in front of him that he hadn't noticed the Marine standing off to the side. His eyes went wide as the Marine's head floated up next to the Boss.

The Omega leaned over and whispered something into the Marine's ear. The Boss extended an open palm and he gripped something invisible which had been placed into it. Kalare assumed it was a blaster, and this was confirmed when the Boss reached over and with well-practiced ease adjusted the settings via the buttons she knew to be on the weapon. Kalare held her breath as she worried about what might happen next. Finally, the Boss spoke to the boy again.

"Son—I don't want to hurt you or anyone else, but you have to understand that I'm very powerful and will if I must. Look at that tree over there."

The Boss gestured with the hand which Kalare knew held the blaster. He continued to stare at the boy even as the boy's eyes turned to where the Boss pointed. The tree exploded in a cloud of flying shards that left behind a smoldering stump. The boy startled at the noise. When he turned back to meet the Boss's gaze, it was clear even under the camouflage how his face had become pale. Without knowing the Boss held an invisible weapon, it must have struck the young primitive as being some form of dark magic. The Boss continued to smile benevolently as he spoke.

"Do we understand each other, son? Are you going to bring me to the rest of your people, or do you want to find out what I can do to your leg if that's what I can do to a tree?"

The boy chewed his lower lip for a moment. Then his shoulders slumped and Kalare knew it was over. He nodded and let his gaze drop to the ground. The Boss gently lifted the boy's chin.

"Good decision." The Omega pitched his voice louder. "Everyone—let's get the president on a stretcher and move out. This boy is going to help us find our colonists."

CHAPTER THIRTY-TWO

I just received a message from the Ship.

Imair was awakened by a dull throb in her belly. Her hands attempted to move there to feel for wounds, but they were restrained by straps. There was another set around her shoulders and a third and fourth around her thighs and calves. Her eyes started to adjust to the darkness, and she made out a rough rock wall next to her. She tried to call out for help, but the dryness in her mouth permitted only a meek croak to escape. A face appeared in the gloom above her. It was Rege.

"What exactly are we going to do about you, Imair?"

Imair's heartbeat spiked at the menacing tone of the man's voice. She tried to recall what had happened to her, but all recent events were impenetrable. The last thing she remembered was walking through the jungle and then a flash of intense pain. From there it was a jumble. Had Rege finally executed a coup of some sort? A million fearsome scenarios flooded her mind. She knew she had to try and summon help, but she couldn't grasp coherent thought and instead started to drown in her panic.

Rege looked away for a moment and then back down at her. His icy expression froze the blood in her veins. He turned and walked out of sight without a further word. No sooner had his footsteps faded than a new set approached. Imair's heart threatened to pound its way out of her chest as she wondered who would show up next and with what intent.

The Boss knelt and smiled at her.

Warmly.

Genuinely.

"I'm glad to see you're awake. You're likely feeling a little wonky. They had to hit you with the most potent anesthetic we've got because of the severity of your wounds. So if you're feeling out of sorts, don't worry. It should wear off pretty quickly. Let me get these straps undone. We traversed some tricky terrain getting here, so they secured you tight to be sure you didn't fall out."

The Boss fiddled around her body for a min and then Imair's restraints fell away. Once the last strap was removed, she struggled to sit up. The Omega slid an arm under her shoulders and gently assisted with raising her torso up and then leaning her back against the wall next to her. The cool dampness of the rock penetrated her clothes and she shivered in response. Her hands probed around her belly and came away tacky. Imair discovered the hole in her shirt and the drying blood which surrounded it.

"Wh-wh-what happened?" Her voice was scratchy and weak.

The Boss handed her a canteen. "Here—just take a few small sips. It will help get rid of that cottonmouth. It's another symptom of the anesthetic."

The first sip of water triggered a coughing fit, but Imair kept down a couple of swallows once her coughs subsided. The pain in her belly began to increase. The sensation went hand-in-hand with the fog in her mind dissipating, so she happily accepted the tradeoff. The Boss started his recap.

"There's something about the jungle that's making our sensors unreliable. A young colonist managed to sneak up on us and shoot you with a wooden projectile that punctured a kidney. You were bleeding out pretty bad, but the Marines took great care of you and got you patched up. After we captured the boy, I convinced him to bring us to the rest of his people. We've been waiting forty-five mins for their leader to show up and speak with us. If you hadn't woken up when you did, I was going to have the medic administer a stimulant so you could hear what he has to say for yourself."

"Have you spoken with any of the colonists yet, Boss? What's their story?"

"So far all I've heard is a bunch of mumbo-jumbo about "others" and agitation about how they've let us into their home here in this cave complex. They were about to attack when we approached, but I gave them a demonstration of our power that convinced them that was a bad idea. Even though they look like savages running around half-naked in their animal skins, they remain intelligent and are fully conversant with verbal language. They don't appear to have any technology or written records, so I'm hoping their leader has some form of spoken history he'll be more willing to share than anyone else has been so far."

Imair didn't want to think about what kind of demonstration the Boss might have used to subdue the colonists. She hoped he hadn't killed too many of them in the process. She went to stand, and the Boss extended an arm in support. Even without the aftereffects of the anesthesia, she was disoriented by the lack of light.

"Why is it so dark in here? Why aren't we using any flashlights?"

"Our former colonists have spent so many generations living in these caves that their eyes have adapted to the dark. Too much light makes them uncomfortable and agitated, so I've ordered everyone to just stumble around for now."

Imair's footing became more and more confident as she walked off the lingering effects of the drugs. She considered relaying her experience with Rege to the Boss, but the more she thought about it the worse of an idea it seemed. Had it even happened, or was it all part of the anesthetic's effects? Perhaps her partially lucid subconscious had just dredged up something which had been weighing her down for months. Even if it really had happened, should she trust the Boss with knowledge that her civilian power structure was more fragile than he was likely aware? She pushed the thoughts aside until she could process them further with an entirely clear head.

They made their way through a series of dim tunnels which left her thoroughly disoriented. The only light came from irregularly placed globs of bioluminescent fungus. At one point she bumped up against an invisible human body and assumed it was one of the ChamWare-clad Marines who were rumored to be guarding the Boss. They passed multiple offshoot caverns where clumps of colonists were visible. One small child looked up as they walked by, and Imair barely suppressed a gasp at the sight of huge black pupils which filled the girl's abnormally large brown eyes practically to overflowing.

They arrived at a cavern large enough to hold at least a thousand people. The Marines and other members of their landing party milled about over to one side. A smaller group which included Sergeant Bailee and Major Odon stood with a group of Marine lieutenants and sergeants as well as a group of colonists. As they approached, Imair noticed that Zax and the female cadet they traveled with during the Revolution were there as well. The group made room for Imair and the Boss to join a semicircle which faced an older colonist. The man's smooth skin and taut muscles contradicted the age suggested by his stark white hair. The Omega spoke.

"Thank you for waiting. This woman is our leader, and I wanted her to hear what you have to share. Please tell us everything you know about how your people came to be on this planet and live here underground."

The white-haired man wore a guarded expression, but he started to speak.

"I don't know this word you use, planet, but I can share the story of us. I am the twenty-seventh leader since this cave became the home of us. My scout shared how he encountered you walking on the path from the dark city. The dark city was built by us many generations ago and was our home until monsters arrived one day. They didn't look anything like us, but they spoke our words and told us the dark city was no longer ours. They forced us into the jungle and told us never to return under penalty of death. The monsters have not visited us since, but our scouts keep watch for their return every moment of every day.

"You are not the only others encountered by us. The first group arrived during the time of the tenth leader of us. She welcomed them to live with us until some of us became sick and died. The tenth leader concluded the others were making us ill. She told us the only way for us to survive was to stay away from others. They were forced back toward the dark city by us and never seen again. More others have found us in the time since, but all leaders have never let any others come close to us. Others who listened to instructions to leave never returned. Those who didn't, died. Others have not visited us in my lifetime until you. None of us have ever heard talk of others who can destroy with their minds alone, though. That power is why you still breathe and the only reason you are in this cave with us and not dead like all the others who wouldn't heed warnings from us."

Imair was curious about one thing. "You say the monsters came and told your people to leave the city. Do your stories say what those monsters looked like?"

"Yes. They were twice as big as the tallest of us. They were red and green with two arms and four legs and eyes which covered their heads."

The Boss caught Imair's attention with a cocked eyebrow. She nodded and the man turned to the colonist.

"This has been interesting to hear. Thank you for sharing. I'm glad your people recognize my power. I don't want to use it to harm any of you, but I will if I have to. Please leave now so that we may talk amongst ourselves and decide what we want to do next."

The white-haired man nodded his assent and walked away along with the rest of the colonists. Once they were out of earshot, Imair addressed the Boss.

"What do you make of that story, Boss?"

"The ants must have visited this continent when they first arrived on the planet. The warriors showed up and probably killed a bunch of colonists, so the rest scattered in a dozen different directions. They settled down in isolated groups, and every once in a while those groups would stumble upon each other. This group decided that anyone outside of their tribe is dangerous which explains why that boy shot first when he saw us. A thousand years later, without any technology or ability to support a civilization, it makes perfect sense how they've devolved into small, primitive tribes."

Imair paused for a moment to consider the Boss's words. "There's a couple of things that bother me about that interpretation. First off, how do you explain the part of their story where the monsters spoke and explicitly instructed them to leave their settlement?"

"Ma'am—how many times have you given someone a simple order only to see your instructions mangled by the time they were communicated through even two or three different people? These myths of theirs have been told thousands of times through the years. Of course the retellings will eventually involve talking monsters instead of terrified people just running for their lives."

"And you think the different groups really are all descended from the same settlement? Wouldn't the colonists have banded back together after they were first scattered?"

The Boss smiled. "New Marines will sometimes piss themselves when they encounter a warrior ant.

How do you think colonists without any weapons or means to protect themselves would react to their appearance? I'm sure the Colonial Security force did a good job of sticking together, but the civilians would have just run for their lives and not stopped until they were thoroughly lost. With all due respect, ma'am."

Imair didn't think the Boss intended any insult, but she was unable to suppress a momentary flash of anger from the obvious bias embedded in his explanation. Major Odon's eyes lit up at her reaction, and she immediately regretted giving the Marine any further ammunition to feed his disrespect. She was attempting to formulate the best response when the Boss closed his eyes for a moment and the blood drained from his face.

"What is it, Boss?"

"I just received a message from the Ship. They're under attack."

CHAPTER THIRTY-THREE

We're too far away and there's not enough time.

"*R*epeat your last, Mini-Boss."
        "*Boss—a massive spacecraft of unknown origin has jumped into the system. They have not launched any fighters yet, but there are inbound kinetic weapons that will hit us in two hundred and seventy-seven secs. I've set Condition One, the FTL drive is spun up, and we're prepared to exit the system.*"

        The Boss opened his eyes for a moment while he considered the situation. Imair looked at him expectantly, as did the others who had gathered around to listen to the colonists' leader. The course of action was clear and he relayed his orders to the Ship.

        "*Mini-Boss—stay where you are until there are only fifteen secs to impact. Then, hit them with a full* spread of torpedoes and jump to the emergency rendezvous. I need them focused on you as long as possible so we can get on the shuttle and off the surface while you're still here to occupy their attention."

"Aye-aye, Boss."

The Boss dropped his connection to the Ship and pinged Major Eryn.

"Major—are you aware of the situation in orbit?"

"Yes, sir. We're ready to depart. Everyone is on board and accounted for except those who are with your team. We can prep the other shuttle while we wait for you and get out of here as soon as you return."

"Negative, Major. We're too far away and there's not enough time. We need extraction at current location. We'll all jam on to a single shuttle. I need you here in one hundred and fifty secs."

The Boss didn't wait for confirmation from Eryn and instead opened his eyes and pitched his voice as loud as possible. The cave provided natural amplification that allowed his message to reach everyone.

"The Ship is under attack. Major Odon—take your Marines and get to the surface. Use your blasters to clear enough jungle so a shuttle has room to land. You have one hundred and forty secs to make it happen!"

Major Odon took off at a furious sprint before the last echo of the Boss's words had faded. His lieutenants, sergeants, and the rest of Charlie Company followed a split-second behind. The Boss waited until they cleared the chamber and then addressed the remaining Crew.

"Look around and be sure we're not leaving anything modern behind. Form up at the exit to this chamber and wait for the order to move."

The colonists milled around and some were clearly agitated by the Crew's activity. The Boss scanned the cavern and estimated how many there were. Bailee waited for orders, and the Boss addressed him with a whisper.

"Sergeant—I want you and a part of your detail on point with me and the rest taking up the rear. Split up the special squad between the two positions. We can manage things if this group of colonists gets out of hand, but if many more show up it will get ugly and we don't have time to waste."

"Yes, sir."

Bailee turned and walked away to give his waiting team their orders. Ten secs later he gave the Boss the ready signal and the Omega called out.

"Everyone—move out. Double-time!"

Bailee set the pace and the Boss fell in behind him. All of the Marines had activated their tracking systems as soon as they entered the warren of tunnels. This allowed the Boss full faith that Bailee was navigating them directly back to the surface even though they took a dozen seemingly random turns. Clusters of colonists lined the route, but they all stood off to the side and allowed the Crew an unmolested passage out of their cave. The Boss was prepared to kill as many as needed if they interfered with the evacuation, but violence proved unnecessary.

Seventy-five secs after he first ordered the Marines to the surface, the Boss and Bailee turned a final corner and stumbled into blinding sunlight. The cave entrance had originally sat in the dark under the impenetrable jungle canopy, but when a Marine company put their efforts into creating an evac zone they were incredibly effective. The air reeked of smoke from hundreds of stumps which smoldered around the new clearing. There was already just about enough space, so the Marines were certain to create a sufficient landing zone before Major Eryn arrived.

The Boss continued to shield his eyes with his hands and turned to watch as Crew spilled out of the cave entrance. More than a few tripped and fell due to the glaring light after so much time away from the sun, but his Plug eventually showed all green when everyone in the landing party was present and accounted for. Imair stood off to his right and waited with her eyes closed. She appeared pained and winded, but she had kept pace with him every step of the mad dash out of the cave. The Boss was impressed.

He checked his Plug. It had been one hundred and thirty secs since he had given his evacuation orders. Just like clockwork, the drone of the shuttle's engines in the distance announced its approach. The Boss called up to the Ship.

"Mini-Boss—sitrep?"

"Nothing about our situation has changed, Boss. The spacecraft is still inbound and they have not launched any craft."

"Excellent. We're within thirty secs of extraction and takeoff. If we don't get to the emergency rendezvous within the next one hundred and twenty mins, you will take my position and advise the civilians to consider us killed in action and tell them to move on."

There was a long silence as the Boss's words sank in. Eventually, the Mini-Boss replied.

"Aye-aye, Boss. Stay safe. See you at the rendezvous."

Who knew what moving on for the Ship would even mean at this point. The Boss was certainly unsure what he might advise Imair to do next if they managed to get off this rock and back up to the Ship. *When* they got off this rock, he corrected as he allowed himself a relieved smile at the sight of Major Eryn's shuttle preparing to land. He was about to order everyone to form up and prepare to board as fast as possible when an inconceivable sound distracted him. The Boss tried to rationalize the noise away as anything other than what it had to be, but that proved impossible.

Another craft was approaching their position.

From behind.

And it was coming in fast.

CHAPTER THIRTY-FOUR

Would you like to speak with him?

Zax picked up on the noise just as the Boss's head started to turn. He was swiveling his around in the same direction to identify the sound when something bright streaked across his field of vision.

The shuttle was hovering a couple of hundred meters above them as it prepared to descend for pickup. The bright streak was a missile that struck the shuttle midship. For a split-sec Zax dared to hope the craft had effectively swallowed the projectile without significant harm, but then a series of secondary explosions bloomed and tore the shuttle apart. Zax loosed an agonized cry at the realization Mase was at its controls and going down with the doomed machine.

Fiery debris began to rain down, and Zax scrambled along with everyone else for the cover of the cave entrance. He found himself in a tight knot of Crew up against Bailee and the Boss. The Marine bled profusely from his scalp but spoke calmly to the Omega.

"Sir—I saw that Major Eryn ejected the flight deck as the shuttle disintegrated. I've sent a squad to see if they survived. I never got a look at whatever took them down, but I heard it fly off in the direction it came from."

"That's good news, Sergeant." The Boss paused for a couple of secs and then continued. "I just heard from Odon. Charlie Company has some light injuries from the debris, but they're all alive. They've taken cover in the jungle on the other side of the landing zone and are awaiting orders."

Sergeant Bailee pointed at Zax and then at something behind him. Zax turned and discovered Kalare was right there. She stood with Aleron and the rest of the engineering team. He had wanted to grab her earlier while they all sat around waiting for the colonists' leader, but she talked with Aleron the entire time. Regardless of the bully's newfound humanity, Zax was unable to approach the two of them together. The Marine spoke.

"Whether we find Major Eryn or not, we've still got these two who can fly the other shuttle. I recommend we send them along with a platoon from Charlie Company to go and bring it back for the rest of us."

The Boss shook his head. "No, Sergeant. When that shuttle takes off it needs to get off this planet immediately before it winds up destroyed as well. We all must go together."

It was the Marine's turn to appear dubious. "With all due respect, sir, that will take forever given the size of this group and the terrain between here and there. Will the Ship wait for us?"

The Boss shook his head again. "I just tried hailing them. They've left the system as instructed. If we don't get to the shuttle fast enough to meet them at the emergency rendezvous, I've given orders to assume we're dead and they should leave."

Zax's emotions were being tossed to and fro. He found himself taken aback by the depths of his feelings regarding Mase—first his despair at assuming the boy had been killed and then his joy at hearing he might have survived. That joy was tempered as he listened to the Boss and then contemplated their situation and the likelihood of spending the rest of his life on this planet. A short time ago he would've been excited to live in the paradise around him, but that was before they had been attacked. Between the ants on the other continent and whatever unknown alien species had just destroyed their shuttle on this one, this place was no longer living up to its high habitation rating.

In the shadows, on the other side of the Boss and the other members of the Crew who were milling around, lurked the young colonist who had shot Imair.

The presence of the boy triggered an idea, and Zax pointed at him and called out to the Omega.

"Boss—why don't we ask the colonist if there's a faster path for getting back to the shuttle?"

The young colonist's brown eyes went wide when he recognized Zax was talking about him. He turned to flee but stopped short as if he had walked into an invisible wall. He was lifted off his feet and a moment later a Marine lifted the visor on her ChamWare and spoke.

"I was keeping a close eye on this one, Boss, after what happened earlier. Would you like to speak with him?"

The Boss smiled. "Well done, Marine. Bring him here."

The colonist had clearly learned the futility of struggling during his earlier capture, and he didn't bother trying to escape. The Marine placed him back on the ground and walked him toward the Boss. She remained invisible other than her face, but indentations were visible from where the Marine's grip held firmly around the fleshy part of the boy's arm. She maneuvered the boy in front of the Boss, released his arm, and dropped her visor. Zax assumed she stayed nearby in case the colonist attempted to bolt again.

The Boss raised his arm toward the boy like he had earlier when he destroyed the tree. Zax was certain the man no longer held an invisible blaster, but the boy was clueless about that and the gesture had the desired effect as his legs began to tremble.

"You remember what I did earlier, son? I'm only going to ask you this question once, so I better believe your answer. Is there a faster route to the dark city than going back the way we came with you the first time?"

Zax empathized with the colonist as he well understood what it was like to feel the weight of the Boss's unspoken threats. The boy paused for a couple of secs and then bit his lower lip and nodded his head.

"Good decision yet again, son. Can you describe it to us so we can get there on our own?"

This time the boy shook his head. "It's underground. The emergency exit for us. It's much faster and will put you out near the edge of the jungle just outside the dark city. I will take you there."

The Boss nodded and then turned to Bailee. "Any word on Major Eryn?"

"Yes, sir. They recovered her and the cadet who was co-piloting with her. Minor injuries—they'll be fine. No other survivors from the shuttle."

The Boss closed his eyes for a moment and then replied. "Thank you, Sergeant. I've instructed Major Odon to get back here with his Marines. Please do the same with the Search and Rescue squad. If we don't get to that shuttle fast enough to catch up with the Ship, we might as well trade in our uniforms for animal skins."

CHAPTER THIRTY-FIVE

What's the information worth to you, Boss?

The acrid smoke hit Imair as soon as she exited the tunnel and emerged into the jungle. It only intensified as the vegetation began to thin out and they approached the edge of the abandoned colony. No one said a word, but it was clear from their sullen expressions that everyone understood what they were likely to find when they reached the landing pad. As they came out from below the last of the jungle canopy, the young colonist approached the Boss with his hand over his eyes to shield them from the sunlight.

"Am I free to go? The jungle is safest for us, especially in the brightness of the day."

"You are."

The boy turned to leave but the Boss called out and signaled for him to wait. The Omega swung his kit bag off his shoulders and rummaged around inside for a few secs. Eventually his hand emerged with a pair of tinted goggles. The Boss approached and extended the strap around the boy's head and settled the lenses over his eyes. The colonist had appeared frozen in fear when the Boss first approached, but his body language switched when the man stepped away. His eyes were wide with excitement—an expression only possible due to the heavy tint of the goggles.

The Boss smiled at him. "Thank you for your help. We are indebted to you."

Without a word, the boy spun and bolted back toward the tunnel entrance. Imair approached and spoke softly to the Boss.

"That sort of kindness is unlike you. I thought we wanted to be certain we left nothing modern behind?"

"I'm not always a heartless monster, Madam President. Besides—I have a sneaking suspicion based on the column of smoke over there that we might be on this planet for the rest of our lives. Making friends with the locals might pay off. Come on—let's go see what fate has in store for us."

The Boss turned to leave and Imair walked alongside as they entered the colony. It was almost as if he was treating her like an equal. A few mins and a half dozen turns later the group established a clear line of sight to the landing pad and confirmed what they had all expected. The second shuttle was a burning, twisted pile of wreckage. Shoulders slumped and muttered curses passed the lips of many. The Boss allowed the reactions to continue for a min and then stood tall with his shoulders back and faced the group with a look of fierce determination.

"We've been hoping for a different outcome, but you're all too smart to be surprised by the scene in front of us. It's done. We can't change it. This planet is our new reality. Crew from Flight can ask any of the Marines, and they'll be happy to share how there are far, far worse places to get stranded.

"I need time to discuss all of this privately with President Imair. Once the President and I are done, we'll meet with the rest of the senior leadership so all of you stay close. We're going to figure out what comes next. In the meantime, we need to be safe and prepare.

"Major Odon—have your Marines establish a perimeter and a watch rotation. Send a platoon to search the colony for items that might prove useful for long-term survival. The original colonists left a lot of useful stuff behind, so let's be sure we don't make the same mistake. Everyone else—use the time to rest. We're going to be busy for a long while. Any questions?"

There were none so the Boss gestured for Imair to follow him toward the administration building. She started walking but stopped and turned when a voice called out behind her.

"Boss—a question, please?"

It was the female cadet. The one who was always hanging around with Zax. Clare or Kalar or something like that. The Boss smiled. Clearly she was one of his favorites. The cadet spoke.

"Boss—I thought I heard the colonists' leader say they had been warned to stay away from the colony. Wouldn't it be a better idea for us to make camp elsewhere?"

"I actually haven't said anything yet about us making camp here, Kalare. We need time to plan right now, and this is the best place to do it. It has great cover and is defensible for a group as well-armed and prepared as we are. All that said, please don't tell me you're worried about the superstitious ramblings of some primitive. We've surveyed the planet extensively. We know the ants are on the other continent, and they have no means of getting from there to here."

The cadet looked at the ground sheepishly as she replied, "Yes, sir. Sorry to bother you, sir."

The Boss turned once again toward the administration building and Imair quickened her pace to get next to him.

"You treated her a little harshly there, Boss."

"I appreciate that input, ma'am. I've spent a lot of years mentoring cadets, and I believe I've gotten pretty good at it. That's the exact message she needed at that moment."

Imair dropped the topic. Her energy was better saved for the difficult discussions she suspected were coming next. They entered the building, and the Boss gestured for her to sit. He did the same. She waited in silence for a few mins until it became unbearable.

"What are you thinking, Boss?"

"I'd like to put that question back to you, ma'am. I'm curious that you aren't more concerned about what we're facing here."

"I'm far more worried about how we'll survive the next few hours than how we'll survive in the long term. Aren't you worried about whoever destroyed the shuttle coming back here to finish the job?"

"Our experience, Madam President, is that most aliens don't worry about tracking down small bands of individuals. They focus on destroying technology first and then dealing with large settlements. The most reasonable expectation if these aliens decide they want to stay in this system is they will deal with the ants first. Therefore, I'm guessing we have weeks to sort out our long-term survival strategy."

"That makes sense. You seemed shocked when the shuttle got destroyed. Did the Ship not warn you there was a hostile craft inbound?"

"That's one thing giving me pause, ma'am. The Ship told me the alien spacecraft had not launched any fighters. They must have some form of advanced technology that allows them to evade our sensors."

"Do you think advanced technology also explains how they got down here and found us so quickly? I may have lost track of time, but I'm almost positive it was less than three min from when their ship jumped into the system until that missile destroyed the shuttle. That's almost an impossible amount of time in which to launch and get down here from orbit, isn't it?"

"Yes, Madam President. I concluded that myself but haven't wanted to alarm anyone who might not have noticed. This is clearly a species with great capability and—"

There was a knock at the door and Major Odon entered.

"Sir—we have a colonist who approached one of our guards and demanded to speak with our leader."

"What? I thought they never traveled out of the jungle in the sunlight."

"It isn't one from the group we were just with, sir. This woman is wearing a standard colonial uniform and her eyes are normal. Shall I bring her in?"

The Boss gaped at Imair. "Ma'am—this strikes me as pretty odd. Even if this is indeed a different tribe, how would they still have uniforms after all this time living away from the colony? We don't have time for this, but we should be sure we understand what's going on around here."

"I agree. Bring her in, Major."

Major Odon made a face like he had just swallowed something rotten when he received the order from Imair, but she couldn't care less. The Boss had done a good job of helping her earn the respect of the Flight staff since the Revolution, but clearly work remained with the Marines. Did it really matter? Even as good as her relationship with the Boss had become, it was probably a safe bet her days in a leadership role were numbered if the planet indeed became their permanent home.

A min later the door opened again and a female colonist was led in by two Marine sergeants. The Boss turned and his face paled. He tried to recover his composure quickly, but Imair was unconvinced. Her lack of conviction was only furthered by the tenor of his voice when he addressed the Marines.

"You're dismissed, Sergeant."

"But, sir, the major instructed us to remain with you for security purposes."

"Get out, Sergeant. That's a direct order."

The Marines turned and left without a further word in response to the magic phrase. Imair found herself holding her breath as the Boss and the colonist stared each other down. Finally the woman spoke.

"I never thought I would see you again. I promised myself I would kill you if that ever proved false, but your goons did a great job searching me and took all my weapons."

Imair was dumbfounded. "Wait—you two know each other? How is that possible? This colony was established more than a thousand years ago."

"She wasn't part of this colony, ma'am. She was chief of colonial security at a different colony we established roughly two years ago in Ship time. You might remember it—the first planet we found after the interstellar desert. How the hell did you get here, Chief?"

"What's the information worth to you, Boss?"

"Chief—I can't fault your anger about what led to your Culling, but I don't have time for games right now."

"Well, Boss, I feel like I have all the time in the world. I guess we've got ourselves a stalemate."

The Boss stared at the woman. Imair was amazed by his calm demeanor, especially as compared to his initial reaction upon the woman's arrival. Finally he spoke.

"A trip back to the Ship along with restoration of rank and position in the Crew. That's my final offer. Take it or leave it."

The woman grinned. "That's exactly what I had in mind, Boss. I'm glad we've managed to see things eye-to-eye. You might want to have a seat because you aren't going to believe what I have to say." The Boss waved off her suggestion and the woman continued. "Ants showed up one day. We were shocked because we knew the Captain had nuked their continent before settling us. That surprise was nothing compared to what happened next.

"A group of warriors approached and first they killed the handful of idiots who tried to fight them off. Typical ant stuff like we've all seen in the training. Fast. Scary. Deadly. But then they herded all of us together and one of them walked up to me and started to speak. I almost fell over. It told me we were being brought back together with our kind. Then we were herded on to a huge ship. A ship! We've never seen *any* technology from the ants, right? We get on this massive transport, and the next thing we know they're filling it up with gas that knocks us all out cold. I woke up feeling heat on my face and found myself lying in the grass with some new sun shining down on me. That was here, fifteen days ago."

The Boss stared at her and Imair went slack-jawed in disbelief. Her head spun with the ramifications of what a story like this meant from a reliable witness. Not only were the ants sentient and capable of human speech, but they were also rounding up the Ship's colonies and consolidating them on this planet for some unknown purpose. She had a million questions but didn't know where to begin. The Boss finally broke the silence.

"So why did you show up here today?"

"We've been staying pretty close to where the ants dumped us. We had all of the food and water we needed, so there wasn't much interest in exploring. I spotted the smoke from that downed shuttle and set off to check it out. When I spotted the Marines in their armor, I realized it was a landing party and decided to try and talk my way back to the Ship. When I saw it was you, well, it would be impossible to measure my excitement. So what's your story? When's the rescue party due with a new shuttle to get us all back up to the Ship?"

The Boss approached Imair, bent over, and spoke softly in her ear.

"Ma'am—I believe we need to fully evaluate the ramifications of this information before we allow anyone else to learn about it. Do you agree?"

Imair nodded and the Boss continued to whisper.

"Give me a few mins alone with the Chief. I need to be certain she doesn't say anything to anyone, and I don't think you want to be around."

Imair stared into the Boss's eyes. She had guessed what his words were suggesting, and the blankness of his expression confirmed her suspicions. She stood to leave.

"Boss—thanks for the information. I need to check in on our rescue, so I trust you can take care of the Chief without me."

Imair walked out without so much as a glance backward. She didn't know what was ahead for all of them based on the new and startling information about the ants, but she knew she definitely wanted nothing to do with what was happening in the building behind her.

CHAPTER THIRTY-SIX

Well, that certainly changes things.

Imair walked out which meant the Boss was inside alone with the colonist who the Marines had led in a few mins earlier. It had only been a quick glimpse, but Zax swore he recognized the woman's face. It didn't make any sense, but he was nearly certain it was the colonial security chief who he and Kalare had delivered a case to on behalf of the Boss years ago. That was obviously impossible, so he kept checking the building entrance to be sure he didn't miss a chance to get a better look.

"Hey, Zax."

It was Mase. The boy had gotten a black eye when he and the Major ejected from the destroyed shuttle. He was also walking with a slight limp.

"Wow—it's great to see you alive, Mase. I've been wondering where you were at."

"The Major and I got checked out by a medic."

The boy gestured to where Major Eryn was sitting on the ground apart from everyone else near the edge of the building. The woman had her head tilted back to soak in the warmth of the sun. A large bandage had been applied to her face.

"You two are lucky to be alive. That was a crazy crash! Did you get a look at whatever shot the missile at you?"

"That's the thing, Zax. What I saw—"

Movement on top of one of the buildings closer to the edge of the jungle caught Zax's attention, and he held up his hand to silence Mase.

"Wait—who is that up there? What are they doing?"

Mase focused on where Zax was pointing. The boy squinted for a sec.

"It looks like that colonist who led us here. The one the Boss gave the goggles to. He's jumping up and down."

The hairs on the back of Zax's neck snapped to attention and, for some unknown reason, he glanced to his left.

Ants!

A dozen red and green warriors were charging toward them in the space between the buildings. All held multiple blades at the ready. Time crawled for Zax and events unfolded in slow motion. He turned to warn the others who relaxed around him. One of the creatures was approaching an unaware Major Eryn.

"Ants! Warriors! All around us!"

After shouting his alert, Zax swung his gaze back in the direction of where the largest group of warriors was bearing down on them. The single ant had indeed grabbed the Major and was dragging her out of sight around the side of the building as she thrashed against its four arms. He screamed again.

"They've got the Major!"

Blaster fire erupted all around Zax and the charging ants fell in a heap before any threw a blade. No sooner had that happened, than multiple groups of the aliens began to emerge from every direction. This only led to a further intensification of the blaster fire directed at them.

Zax scanned the area in a frenzy trying to identify the location of the blasters, but it was impossible to know for sure. The invisible Marines were staying on the move to prevent anyone from tracking their position. What was clear, though, was that it was not some small handful of Marines in ChamWare guarding the Boss. There were at least two dozen blasters laying down sufficient fire to keep the aliens at bay. Sergeant Bailee was suddenly at Zax's side.

"Up against the building, cadet!"

Zax fought the urge to grab his blaster from the kit bag he had dumped in a heap along with all of the other Crew from Flight. Instead, he listened to the

Marine and put his faith in the safety of a solid structure at his back and a ring of covering fire from the best Marines on the Ship—the Boss's personal protection detail. He was too afraid to take his eyes off the charging aliens, so he scampered backwards toward the building instead. Zax experienced a small moment of relief a sec later when Major Eryn came running back around the building free of her alien captor. She beat him to the building and slammed her back against it in a spot right next to Imair.

Zax's hand was extended behind him to feel for the building as he got closer and it instead found someone's leg. He turned and met the gaze of the Boss. The man reached out and pulled him by the shoulder up against the building next to him. There was no sign of the colonist the Omega had been with inside the building. Bailee arrived and the Boss peppered him with questions.

"How the hell did this many show up without warning, Sergeant? Where's Charlie Company? How did they let all these ants inside our perimeter?"

"Major Odon insists his Marines had a tight cordon and there's no way they came past them, sir. They're jumping into ChamWare so they can join the fight."

"What's the plan?"

"We're still working on it, sir."

"They just keep charging without throwing their blades. It's like they're trying to overwhelm us rather than kill us."

Zax had noticed the same thing about the aliens' pattern. Bailee replied.

"We can keep mowing them down like this for a while, but eventually we're going to run out of ammo." The Sergeant closed his eyes for a moment and then reopened them. "Charlie Company is on the way. We're going to form a gauntlet that lets us get out of the colony and back into the jungle, so we can make a dash for the colonists' cave system. We can defend that entrance a lot easier than all of this space, and if it gets bad enough we can use explosives to seal the bugs out altogether."

While they waited for the Marines to arrive, the sights of the battle drove Zax's fear and agitation ever higher. The impossibly fast, scurrying movements of the creatures triggered a deep revulsion within him, but his eyes remained locked on the horrifying scene out of morbid curiosity. Wave after wave of the aliens charged at the Crew's invisible ring of protection only to be taken down by the Marine's precision blaster fire. The next line of ants would grab their fallen comrades and pull them away to clear the path for the group who replaced them from behind. It was a relentless and never-ending pattern, and Zax became increasingly hopeless about their prospects.

The Boss jerked suddenly against him, and Zax discovered the man had craned his body to get a better view around the side of the building. He followed the Omega's gaze and a moment later witnessed a miraculous sight. A formation of fighters from the Ship was coming in fast and low toward the colony. Right behind them was a shuttle! The Boss pointed and called out.

"Bailee—look!"

The Sergeant turned and a tight smile formed on his mouth. "Well, that certainly changes things." He closed his eyes and then reopened them. "New plan. Charlie Company is making their way around to the landing pad. Boss—call those fighters in to provide covering fire and tell them to keep the ants at bay so we can join the Marines for extraction."

"Roger that, Sergeant."

Twenty secs later the cacophony of blaster fire was replaced by something that made Zax's ears hurt worse even as it warmed his heart. The fighters hovered over their position and unleashed volley after volley from their ion cannons at the charging ants. The aliens kept coming, but the intense wall of heavy fighter ordnance slowly pushed them back further and further. Bailee called out to everyone above the din.

"Leave everything behind and get to the landing pad. Now!"

Zax didn't need to be told twice. He tucked his head and ran. The shuttle finished its descent as he reached the pad and the ramp at its rear opened and discharged a phalanx of Marines. They waved everyone onboard, and Zax kept running full speed up into the belly of the spacecraft. He was soon joined by Kalare and Aleron and then Mase and Major Eryn and finally Imair and Rege along with the rest of the Flight group.

The Boss and Bailee stood by the entrance with Major Odon, and Zax assumed they were counting heads as the ChamWare-clad Marines invisibly hustled up the ramp. After a min the two Marines each gave the Boss a thumbs up, the Omega closed his eyes, and the ramp started to close.

Zax scrambled to a window to get a look outside the craft as they lifted off. The fighters were still hovering on station, but their cannons had gone quiet as the ants acted as if they had declared a retreat. The shuttle climbed higher, and Zax caught a glimpse of a solitary human scampering over the terrain toward the jungle. The colonist stopped and gawked up at the shuttle for moment before resuming the course which had him disappear a few secs later under the dense tree canopy. Zax imagined the stories the boy would share when he returned to his people in their caves, and the vision brought a smile to his face. He only hoped the actions of the Crew in drawing the ants back to the human continent had not doomed their colonists' descendants to extinction.

CHAPTER THIRTY-SEVEN

None of this is getting us anywhere.

As happy as he was to be on a shuttle making its way back to the Ship, the Boss fumed about many of the preceding events. He was surrounded by the senior leadership who had filled the compartment for a debrief. Imair sat across from him, and Sergeant Bailee occupied the chair next to her. Rege leaned up against the bulkhead while Major Odon paced back and forth. Major Eryn was the only one of the bunch who did not appear agitated but instead watched the rest of them with detached bemusement. The Boss assumed she must still be in shock from the crash.

The connection to the Ship went through, and the Mini-Boss materialized on the screen. She saluted the Boss and spoke.

"It's good to see you, sir. Didn't expect to ever do so again."

"I'm curious about that, Mini-Boss. I left you with explicit orders that the Ship was to continue onwards without us if we didn't catch you at the rendezvous point. I never said anything about launching a rescue mission."

"My apologies, Boss. I relayed your instructions to the civilians exactly as ordered but was overruled. They told me they had explicit instructions from President Imair to attempt a rescue at all costs if the need for one arose. They refused any guidance to the contrary, so I put together the plan. Thankfully, the unknown aliens were gone when we jumped back into the system. I'm guessing all of the torpedoes we launched at them earlier dissuaded them from sticking around. We maintained comms blackout until we had you in visual because we didn't want to risk surprise encounters if anyone detected our signals. The vids I saw from the shuttle made it look like we got there just in time."

The Boss was taken by surprise to hear about Imair's orders. He turned to her.

"Madam President—I'm impressed that you left instructions regarding a rescue with your staff before we departed the Ship."

"Thanks, Boss, but I actually didn't. I reached out to them when we learned the Ship was under attack."

"I'm confused, ma'am. I was with you when that information came in. You were never with our comms person from that point forward."

"I'm sorry, Boss, but I thought you knew. I got Plugged In."

The Boss was shocked but fought to maintain a neutral appearance. It was bad enough he was unable to block Imair from communicating with Alpha, but now she had the capability to do so at will and from anywhere. Imair's expression made it clear she knew the Boss would be surprised by the news and suggested she was enjoying his discomfort. Rege appeared positively giddy at the amount of tension in the compartment, and Bailee scrutinized the odious civilian through narrowed eyes. Odon had stopped his pacing and was muttering something that reflected his negative opinion about civilians having Plugs. The Boss wanted to explore this development further, but he put it aside to wait for a better time. He turned back to the screen.

"Thanks for the recap, Mini-Boss. I appreciate you getting us off that rock."

The Boss cut the connection to the Ship and weighed how best to proceed. Imair spoke while he was still formulating his thoughts.

"Major Odon—Your Marines were on guard. How is it that we found ourselves overrun by those bugs with the only warning coming from a cadet?"

The Marine was visibly shocked to have such a direct, public rebuke from Imair, and his cheeks filled with color as his fists clenched. The Boss jumped in to defuse the situation.

"Major—what the President is trying to understand is how you believe the ants were able to evade your perimeter."

The Marine remained red-faced as he replied. "We had a complete 360-degree view around the colony, and there was zero notice of the ants approaching. It was as if they materialized out of thin air. The only thing I can think of is that they were somehow hiding in one of the buildings that we didn't check and clear completely."

Rege guffawed. "Hiding in a building? Did you see how many of those creatures were coming at us? It must have been thousands. Admit it—one of your guards was asleep at her post. The aliens found the weak spot and came marching right in under your nose."

The Marine charged at the civilian and got within centimeters of his face. Spittle flew as he screamed his reply, but Rege did not flinch.

"Asleep? I've been over the vids from all of our helmet cams, and it's clear we remained alert at all times. Our perimeter was intact and never violated. You don't have the slightest clue what you're talking about, but if you'd like to step outside the compartment I'd be happy to educate you."

Rege started to move until the Boss yelled even louder than Odon had.

"Stand down, civilian! You too, Major! None of this is getting us anywhere. Clearly there's something about the bugs' abilities that has changed, and I want all of your vids handed over to the exobiology unit for immediate and priority review. As often as we encounter them, we'd better understand the ants' new capabilities before we get caught by surprise again."

"I agree, Boss." Imair paused and then continued. "I doubt we'll be back down on a planet with any ants at this point, but we should definitely try to be better prepared if it happens. Let's forget about them for a min, though, and talk about whatever aliens attacked the Ship and destroyed our shuttles. Do we think that was the ants finally revealing their technological abilities?"

"I don't believe that's the right conclusion, Madam President. If it was the ants' spacecraft up there, they would have stuck around once we left. Right? Why would they leave after scaring us off with all of their colonists still down on the planet? We surely wouldn't."

"Well, Boss, that isn't entirely true, now is it? We're leaving our colonists behind after an encounter with some aliens."

The Boss grimaced. "I think you know what I meant, ma'am. I need some time to review all of our data so I can be better prepared to answer your questions. May I be dismissed, and we can continue this discussion once we are back on the Ship?"

"Of course, Boss. Thank you."

The Crew walked toward the hatch leaving Imair and Rege behind. As he walked to his private compartment, the Boss received an inbound message on his Plug. It was Alpha.

"I have important information to share, sir."

CHAPTER THIRTY-EIGHT

You were right.

Zax entered the mess hall for dinner and almost bumped into Kalare as she was leaving. They stared at each other awkwardly for a moment until she grinned and spoke.

"That was some trip, wasn't it? I have to stop visiting planets if I'm going to almost get killed every time."

Zax's heart almost burst in response to Kalare's warm tone, and he laughed deeply. "Yeah—what are you...two out of three with near-death experiences on the surface?"

She echoed his laugh, and then they waited in silence again until it became uncomfortable. "Well, I've got to get going."

Zax nodded and, shoulders slumped, started to walk toward the food stations. He hadn't gone two paces before Kalare called out.

"Wait!"

Zax turned back and was enveloped in Kalare's arms. It was so unexpected that his muscles froze, but the shocked paralysis wore off quickly and he soon returned the embrace. They held each other for somewhere between an instant and an eternity. She backed away, and her blue eyes glistened with tears.

"I'm sorry I've shut you out, Zax. I'm just so worried about you getting demoted again, or worse, and I don't know what to do with my feelings. It seemed better for a while to remove the risk of getting hurt by pushing you away intentionally. That's how I lived for all those years before we met, though, and I've realized now I don't want that again. I want us to fix this, OK? Can we talk about it tomorrow morning? Breakfast—just like we always used to?"

There was a lump in Zax's throat, and he only managed a nod in reply. She beamed back at him. It had been far, far too long since he'd seen that glorious smile, and he basked in how good it made him feel. She gave a small wave and walked away.

Zax approached the food station and debated whether he should have nutripellets or solid food. They had jumped away from the planet for safety as soon as the shuttle landed but hadn't yet announced the next Transit. He grabbed heaping portions of his favorites after deciding to treat himself to a real meal after the stress and excitement of the surface trip. He walked to his usual table and attacked the pile of food with gusto.

A few mins later Mase shuffled to the table dragging his injured foot even more than he had down on the planet. Zax greeted him.

"What happened? It looks like you're limping more than you were earlier."

"Yeah—I hurt it even worse when we scrambled to the shuttle. I was afraid of getting left behind and carted away by the ants. The adrenalin kicked in. I'm scheduled at the medbay first thing tomorrow morning."

The boy sat down and stared at Zax for a few secs. He pushed his tray aside and leaned in.

"Zax—you're not going to believe what I have to tell you. I promise that I've checked it fifty different ways. I've confirmed everything. Do you trust me?"

Zax nodded his head, but Mase shook his.

"No, Zax, I really mean it. Do you trust me? With your life? You won't be able to un-know what I'm about to share with you. I don't want to tell you any of it unless you're certain you're ready to believe without hesitation."

"Whoa! That's a pretty tall order. Yes—I trust you, Mase, though I'm likely to have a million questions about anything you tell me which is as serious as you're making this sound. That's because I'm going to need to understand it fully, not because I don't trust you. OK?"

Mase stared at him for a few secs before he finally spoke.

"A while back you told me about the different encounters the Ship has had with unknown spacecraft. You said you believed they were all related to the human fighter from that video you released."

Zax nodded and Mase continued.

"That whole discussion got me wondering about how to prove you were right. And that's what I've done."

Zax's jaw dropped. His heart seemed to pound in his throat, and he found himself unable to breathe as if it were actually blocking his airway. He slowly pushed his tray aside and stared at the boy while saying the only two words possible.

"Tell me."

Mase took a breath and then started.

"You know how I've hacked into the AI that manages the Leaderboard. I've always assumed similar techniques would work for accessing other AIs. I never had good reason for doing so. Until you told me those stories.

"It ended up being a lot harder than I would have guessed. I discovered that all the systems use different security protocols. The complexity and challenge of breaking into them increases exponentially based on the sensitivity of the data involved. I got into the Replicators pretty quickly and had fun making stuff without getting charged for usage."

A group walked by and Mase paused for a moment until they were no longer within earshot.

"My goal was to get into the Threat and Scan and Flight historical records. The detailed history is only accessible if you have a legitimate reason to see it. And we know the Omegas can classify anything they want to hide with even higher levels of security. I figured the only way to really prove or disprove your suspicions was to get full access to all of the low level, raw data records. It was infinitely harder to get those than to crack the Leaderboard. I did it. I was ready to talk about it the other day. You blew me off."

The boy grinned. Zax wanted to punch him, but he maintained his patience and waited for him to continue.

"I figured out how to chain my entry attempts across multiple systems. I linked where I needed to and gained full access to all of the records. You were right. The fighter in your video is the same type of craft that attacked the Ship at the white dwarf star. It's also the same type of craft that was at that planet a few months ago when we jumped out of the system before you had a chance to identify it. And it's also the same type of craft that launched the missile that brought down my shuttle earlier today."

Mase paused to let it all sink in. Zax wanted desperately to breathe, but it was impossible. *You were right.* The words bounced around in his mind. He had always known, but now there was proof. Mase spoke again.

"Wait, wait—there's more! It wasn't a single human fighter that destroyed our tanker and all those fighters at the white dwarf. The records recovered from one of our destroyed fighters revealed that a massive craft entered the system after we jumped out. It was that mothership which destroyed all of ours. That mothership is exactly the same type as the one that attacked the Ship earlier today!"

Zax wanted to scream. Both from anger and excitement. There were two questions left.

"Is it possible to see who accessed this information?"

Mase nodded. "Yes. The Captain and Flight Boss accessed everything about your video and how it related to the ship from the White Dwarf. The Boss also reviewed all the information about the planet encounter from a few months ago. He has already viewed the data from today."

"You're absolutely certain about everything you're telling me?"

"Yes. I'd stake both of our lives on it."

CHAPTER THIRTY-NINE

Let's set the course and start tomorrow.

I mair greeted the Boss as he sat down in the seat across the table in her quarters. She pushed her dinner to the side without having had more than a couple of bites.

"Quite a day, don't you think, Boss?"

"Yes, Madam President. It certainly was."

Imair gave the Boss a good, long look, and he met her gaze without so much as an extra blink. "What can I do for you tonight? As you can imagine, I'm feeling pretty worn out. The folks in medbay told me I should try to spend some extra time in bed the next few days."

"A couple of items, ma'am. I'm curious why I wasn't part of the discussion when you decided to get Plugged In."

"Do you think I should have asked for permission?"

"Certainly not, ma'am. You're in charge and can do as you see fit. I just would have expected that I'd be informed. If nothing else, we could have been communicating by Plug all of this time."

"It's good to hear you reinforce that I'm in charge, Boss. Major Odon and a number of his Marines don't appear to exactly agree with that assessment. In fact, word from Rege is they almost let me bleed out when I got shot."

The Boss shook his head. "Ma'am—I'd advise you to not seek any amount of self-worth based on the opinion of Marines. There is no one a Marine truly respects other than another Marine. There have been plenty of times when they've expressed opinions about me as negative as they hold for you right now."

"Fair point, I suppose. Anything else bothering you?"

"Yes, ma'am. I'm worried you were issuing critical orders to the Ship about emergency procedures without consulting me first. I've always understood your intent was to allow me to continue to keep us safe. That's hard for me to do if you've issued orders I'm not aware of. Particularly when those orders contravene those I've already given to my staff."

"Here's my challenge, Boss. I totally agree that you know what is best for the Ship based on 5,000 years' worth of Crew experience and training. That experience is missing a critical component, however, and that's how the civilians factor into the equation.

"Now here's where you'll want to tell me that you've had lots of training about civilians. And I know you have, particularly when it comes to controlling them and putting down uprisings. Those are valuable skills, and, frankly, I may ask you to put them to use again on my behalf. For right now, though, I still need to use a softer form of power to influence what is happening with my ten million fellow civilians. You may feel your Mini-Boss would take over without missing a beat if the Ship had left us behind earlier today, but there is no Mini-Imair with anywhere close to the same ability. Without me, it all spins out of control."

"Ma'am—is there anything you've hidden from me about what is happening in the civilian sectors?"

Imair considered whether she should let the Boss into the loop about her concerns around Rege and how they had been further exacerbated down on the planet. It would be a good opportunity to strengthen the trust in their relationship even further, but instead she saved the information for another time.

"I think you have all the knowledge you need around that right now. It bears repeating, though, that I'm very worried about the long-term stability of our civilian population. We've continued to ration out morsels of hope for the past couple of years, and that has kept things from spiraling out of control. But I have tremendous concerns about how they might react to what we learned earlier today."

"Which part, Madam President?"

"That ants are traveling the galaxy and rounding up humans for some unknown reason. Look—there are three positive outcomes to this journey that can solve our civilian problem. The first is if we manage to actually find these other humans and learn they've built a star-faring culture on some amazing planet that can also support the billion inhabitants of our Ship. That outcome would be even better if we were to learn it was Earth which had somehow recovered and was capable once again of supporting life and sending people to the stars."

The Boss interrupted. "Ma'am—you don't seriously believe we would find Earth habitable, do you? We know from our history that its death was imminent when the Ship launched, and it left with the brightest people who might have been capable of saving the planet."

"I know, Boss. I'm not as stupid as I think you give me credit for sometimes. In fact, I don't believe there's any reasonable likelihood we'll ever even find the other humans. My guess is that fighter from the famous video is an incredibly rare specimen whose creators we'd never locate in a billion years of trying. So that leaves us with the final positive outcome as the most likely. We'll eventually return to one of the spectacular planets we've colonized in the past. One of the nines or tens that will support everyone on the Ship. We'll settle it and call it New Earth."

The Boss paused before asking his question.

"Ma'am—if you think that's the most likely outcome, why don't we just take that course right now? I wouldn't settle on the planet we just left given what we've learned about the ants, but there are others within a few years' journey which are equally attractive."

"It's a question I've been wrestling with, Boss. I think it boils down to one word—hope. My Revolution got its start when that video made its way around the Ship, and people got it into their heads that we were no longer alone. A feeling of belonging is a powerful weapon, and a hope to find others from our tribe became a key part of how we made people believe in our uprising. What made that hope particularly powerful was the image from that video which showed the picture of Earth.

"Perhaps people from the Crew see pictures of our homeworld frequently as part of your coursework, but prior to that video most civilians had never uttered the word Earth, much less seen an honest-to-goodness picture of it. If finding other humans was the spark for our Revolution, then potentially finding them back home on Earth was the fuel that fed its fire."

Imair stood to finish her thought. Her belly was starting to throb again and she found that standing was slightly more comfortable than sitting.

"If my people lose their hope, then I fear we'll all be in trouble since hopeless people are the most dangerous people. I'm confident we can eventually replace the hope for other humans and the hope for Earth with a new hope for a New Earth, but we need time for the situation to improve for everyone before we attempt that transition."

"That makes sense, ma'am. You've mentioned the importance of hope before, but this puts it all in much better context. It also explains why you've held back on the news you haven't been willing to share with all of the civilians."

"With all of that in mind, Boss, what would you advise we do now?"

The Boss was quiet for a couple of min and Imair grabbed a piece of fruit which she tossed from hand to hand while she waited. She eventually tired of the game and threw the apple into a wastebin just as the Boss finally spoke.

"I've thought things through from every angle, ma'am, and my advice is that we should head directly toward Earth. Checking these old colonies isn't doing anything for us but causing headaches, so let's stop. If our best outcome is to wean civilians off Earth as the answer to their dreams, then let's start that process as fast as we possibly can. I'll work with Alpha to understand which of the colonies closest to Earth represent the highest quality planet for habitation, and we'll be prepared to move onwards as soon as everyone has had a chance to see the deadness of our homeworld with their own eyes."

"I agree. Let's set the course and start tomorrow. We'll need to figure out whether we tell the civilians that we're going to stop checking colonies, or if we keep that hidden. I'm not sure which is the better approach at this point."

A chime signaled that someone was outside. Imair called out permission to enter, but the hatch didn't open and she called out again.

CHAPTER FORTY

I can take care of what's needed next.

Zax's hand was poised above the handle. His legs shook and his heart beat furiously. There was no going back once he walked through the hatch, so he took a couple of extra beats to be certain of his resolve. He finally pushed it open, entered, and immediately regretted his decision.

The Boss was in the compartment with Imair.

"Hello, Zax." The Boss smiled at Zax as he rose from his chair. "I assume you came to her quarters for President Imair, and you don't need me for anything."

Zax's mouth had gone bone dry at the sight of the Boss, but thankfully the man's implied question must have been rhetorical as he turned back to Imair without waiting for any answer.

"Get some rest over the next few days, ma'am. I can take care of what's needed next."

The Boss turned and walked out. The hatch shut behind him and Zax was alone with Imair. She sat down.

"Hello, Zax. Please forgive me if I act restless while we speak. I'm uncomfortable when I sit and uncomfortable when I stand, so I'm trying to figure out which position is the least worst. What can I do for you?"

Even as the civilian smiled at him, Zax's resolve wavered. Was he doing the right thing? Was she someone who wanted to serve and protect *everyone* on the Ship, or just another partisan playing for power? Sometimes working with the Boss and sometimes against him depending on her own needs of the moment? There was only one way to find out. With one last deep breath, Zax charged full speed into the unknown.

"The Ship has repeatedly encountered human spacecraft. This includes the fighter that destroyed the shuttle and its mothership which attacked the Ship earlier today. The Boss has known since the very beginning and has kept it hidden from everyone except the Captain. I think he tried to kill me and my friend Kalare two years ago to keep the truth hidden. I believe the only reason I'm still alive is because I released the video of the human fighter I discovered. Once it was out there, they couldn't very well kill me because it would look too suspicious."

Imair stood up. She waited for a few secs as she bobbled on her feet, and then sat down. She moved to try standing again, but then she leaned back instead. She took a long drink from her glass of water before pointing at the seat the Boss had just vacated.

"Sit down, Zax. Let's start from the very beginning. Talk to me like I don't know anything because there's a good chance I don't know a lot of what you're going to tell me."

"Yes, ma'am. May I have a drink first? I'm pretty nervous."

Imair handed Zax her glass and he finished the rest of her water. He wiped a few stray drops off his lips with a trembling hand and then dove into his story.

"A little more than two years ago, I was working in Flight Ops when the Ship encountered an unknown spacecraft. The pilot who investigated the craft reported that it appeared human in origin, but the Ship left the system before there was confirmation. When we returned a tanker and eleven fighters had been destroyed. We were told that Alpha reviewed all of the available data and confirmed the spacecraft was indeed unknown and not human. That was a lie."

After that preamble, Zax next shared what happened during the fateful Landfall two years ago when he found the abandoned human fighter on the planet with the carnivorous trees. Imair's eyes went wide when he described how he stumbled upon the craft.

"I'm confused, Zax. I've known you were the one who released the video but understood it was a Flight officer who found the fighter. Is that inaccurate?"

"Her name was Lieutenant Mikedo. She was with me on the planet and told me to never admit to anyone how I made the discovery. Mikedo claimed that she found it because she was afraid the news about its existence would be dangerous."

"Why dangerous?"

"She feared that news about other humans would be enough to tip all of you civilians into massive unrest. Of course, she was correct. She was also right to fear the information was worth killing to keep it a secret. She died within mins of reporting the discovery to the Boss."

"Zax—you mentioned there were hostile aliens on that planet. What species?"

"The ants, ma'am."

Imair paused for a moment before asking what happened next.

"Kalare and I were sent down to the colony on a secret mission for the Boss. While we were there, one of the colonists tried to kill us. He was doing it for someone on the Ship who guaranteed he could use our shuttle to get back on board. Only the Boss knew we were going, ma'am. He was there waiting when our shuttle returned and seemed surprised when we were still on board."

"If you believed the Boss was trying to kill you because you knew his secret, why did you turn around and share it with everyone? Didn't you worry he would kill you anyway?"

"I did, ma'am, but Mikedo convinced me otherwise. She sent me a message right before she died, and I didn't get to read it until much later. She said the best way to save my life was to make the secret worthless. Once everyone knew about the fighter, there wouldn't be anything worth killing me over."

Imair stood, remained steady after doing so, and started to pace. "So, then we encountered them again today?"

"Actually, ma'am, there was another encounter. Do you recall the last colony we visited before this one? The day you talked to me about Nolly and then we spotted an inbound bogey and jumped out of the system?"

"That was a human fighter?"

Zax nodded. "It was. It was highly unusual for the Boss to jump us out of a system without first identifying an unknown craft, and now I know why he did it. He must have suspected and wanted to leave before I had a chance to identify it."

"And now, today?"

"Yes, ma'am. I have confirmation the fighter that shot down our shuttle was the same type I found on that first planet. Furthermore, the mothership that forced the Ship to leave the system is the same type of spacecraft that destroyed our tanker and all our fighters three years ago."

"And you're absolutely certain about all of this information? You have proof of some sort?"

"Yes, ma'am."

"And that includes how the Boss is definitely aware of it all?"

Zax nodded.

Imair was silent for a few mins before sitting back down in her chair. "OK, cadet. Thank you for sharing. Does anyone else know about all of this?"

Once again, Zax was prepared to lie to not involve anyone else. "No, ma'am."

"Let's keep it that way. My pain meds are starting to wear off, and I'm having a hard time following along right now. Let me sleep on this information overnight, and then we can take care of what to do about it tomorrow. OK?"

"Yes, ma'am."

Zax rose and Imair extended her hands and took Zax's in hers. "I know this was hard for you to do, but it was absolutely the right thing. I believe you may very well have saved the Ship by coming to me with this. Thank you."

The adrenalin rush had subsided, and Zax risked keeling over from exhaustion. Without the energy for further speech, he simply nodded and turned to leave. He caught Imair's reflection in a mirror as he approached the hatch. She must have been equally tired since she sat still with her eyes closed. It was almost as if she had a Plug and was communicating

with someone, but of course that was impossible for a
civilian.

CHAPTER FORTY-ONE

It must be a mistake.

Zax woke at reveille, but instead of getting up right away he accepted the hit of twenty demerits and remained in bed for a few extra mins. After all, he'd just get Mase to add them back later. He finally peeled himself off his bunk and made his way toward the showers.

As he walked through the berth, he noticed two armed Marines milling around. With all of the excitement, Zax had totally forgotten about the Cull. Like clockwork, the lowest performers across the Ship were being rounded up and marshaled to the cryostorage holds. They would be put on ice until they eventually woke up far in the future as part of some hideous colony. Though, with the Ship having dropped its original Mission and no longer establishing colonies, who knew when any of those who had been Culled would get their chance to live again.

One of the Marines made eye contact with Zax as he approached. He closed his eyes for a moment and then reopened them and held out his hand to block Zax's path.

"Cadet Zax—come with us."

Zax's first instinct was to ignore the Marine and walk on past. Perhaps Mase had put these two up to giving him a heart attack. He went to brush aside the first Marine and the second reached out and grabbed Zax's upper arm in a vise-like grip.

"Wait—what are you doing? I'm at the top of my class! There's been a mistake...look!"

Zax pointed to the Kappa Leaderboard with his free hand, and his mouth fell open. His name sat at the bottom of the list. His score had dropped 95 percent from when he went to sleep last night!

What?

How?

Who?

He pinged Mase via his Plug.

"Good morning, Zax. I can't talk right now. I'm walking into the medbay."

"Mase—I'm about to get Culled! Look at my Leaderboard score. What happened?"

"What? That's crazy. It must be a mistake. Hold on."

There was no activity for a moment as Mase used his Plug to access the Leaderboard system. While

Zax waited for the boy to reply, the Marine gave him a yank on his arm to get him moving. They left the berth as the other cadets stared wide-eyed in wonder at the sight. Zax had been at the top of the Leaderboard for years, and his scoring cushion had only increased in recent months. Everyone was abuzz with ideas as to what happened for him to fall so far without anyone being aware.

Finally, Mase replied. *"I don't know what to tell you, Zax, but this looks legit. It was the Boss. He hit you with a massive number of demerits last night after lights out. What did you do? Did you tell someone about what I told you? We agreed you weren't going to do anything with that information until we discussed it some more together."*

"Don't worry, Mase. Your secret is going into cryosleep with me. If they knew about your involvement, wouldn't you have a couple of Marine blasters pointed at you right now too? I'm sorry. I did what I thought was best, and I did it the way I believed would keep you safe. I have to go now. I've got to reach Kalare. Thanks for being my friend and helping me, Mase. Good luck. Don't do anything stupid like I have."

Zax cut the connection before the boy got out another word. He pinged Kalare next.

"Hey Zax! I'm here in the mess hall. Where are you? Are you taking an extra-long shower again? Don't you think it's a little creepy talking to me when you're naked in the shower? It's our first meal together

in months and you're making me wait? If I didn't know any better—"

"Kalare—shut up! I'm getting Culled!"

"What? This isn't the least bit funny, Zax."

"I'm not joking! There are two marines with blasters at my back, and they're walking me to cryostorage processing."

"Wait! This must be a mistake. I'm pinging the Boss...he can fix it!"

Zax grimaced at her mention of the man. What would Kalare think when she learned it was the Boss who had caused this? He was figuring out how to break that news when the connection went dead. He tried again but was unable to reach her. He quickly determined his Plug had been reduced to limited functionality. No messaging and no interaction with Ship systems. He was cut off.

As they walked the hallways, a few Crew gawked at the sight. None of them knew who he was, but rather they were just reacting to being so close to anyone who was on his way out of their world. Thankfully, the majority of people they encountered were civilians who looked away instead. He appreciated the manner in which they gave him his dignity by not treating him as a sideshow.

A million thoughts flooded Zax's mind. Many of them centered on the Boss. Zax had clearly chosen the wrong path in delivering the information to Imair. He had believed she would be appalled by the man's actions and would appreciate any assistance in getting him out of the way. Somehow, Zax had dramatically misinterpreted her response.

Or perhaps Imair didn't even know. Was it possible the Boss had her compartment under surveillance? Yes, Zax had told her a lot of information already, but moving him into cryostorage would prevent her from learning anything further. Perhaps Zax wasn't even destined for a colony. It wasn't unheard of for people being Culled to die during cryosleep initiation. A convenient "accident" would remove the ability for the President to get any further information out of Zax permanently.

Regardless of why it had happened, it was done. Zax had clearly deluded himself about having the Boss in his sights. The man had defeated him. The Omega had killed Mikedo, and now he was finishing the job by getting rid of Zax. His shoulders began to slump from the weight of defeat until something lit a spark in his belly.

Irrespective of the outcome, Zax had done his best to avenge Mikedo. He had done so while keeping Kalare safe, and Mase as well. Yes—the Boss was still wreaking his havoc on the Ship, but at least he had been partially muzzled by Imair and the rest of her civilians. The path of the Ship had been changed forever, and it was all due to Zax. And he did it all while also getting into the Pilot Academy and nearly reaching the end of the program at the very top. He refused to go out like a beaten man. He held his head high and stared defiantly at anyone who met his gaze.

After a few mins of walking, they finally reached the cryostorage processing facility closest to the Kappa berth. There were dozens spread throughout the Ship, so each of the Culled could be prepared in relative isolation rather than be herded en masse into a single location after receiving the worst news of their lives. A window revealed that the entry room was currently empty save for a clerk who sat at a workstation. The hatch opened and the Marines led Zax inside.

The clerk looked up and fixed Zax with a blank stare. "Hand."

The man extended his arm toward Zax, palm up. Zax returned the gesture and the man grabbed him by the wrist. The clerk brought his other hand off the workstation and revealed the DNA sampler it held. The device extracted a sample with a slight sting to his finger and a moment later the man's screen flashed green and showed Zax's name.

Echoes of pounding fists and anguished screams suddenly filled the small space. They all turned toward the hatch where Kalare stood on the other side of the window. She tried yanking on the handle repeatedly, but the hatch was security coded and she didn't have access. Her brilliant blue eyes were shot red and tears streamed down her face as she pounded on the transparent titanium.

"You can't do this! He's at the top of his class! You have the wrong person! Take me instead...please...take me!"

Zax's resolve finally shattered and he began to silently weep. One of the Marines grabbed his arm and led him with a jerk past the clerk and through another hatch. He twisted his neck to watch Kalare until they turned the corner, and she was gone from view. Her screams echoed for another few paces and then even those faded away.

They entered a hallway that was lit with a soft red glow. Equally spaced doors on the right and left were each labeled with a name. They walked halfway down until they found the door that bore Zax's name. It slid open automatically to reveal a cryotube with its cover closed and a cryosuit draped across it. The Marine gave him a final push inside, and then the door slid shut behind him. A voice came over a speaker.

"Strip and then don the cryosuit."

Zax did as he was told. He didn't see anything else to do with his clothes so he threw them into a heap in the corner of the small room. The cryosuit was similar to his flight suit in that it had a hood and the back was studded with metal contacts. He pulled the hood over his head, and the suit adjusted until it was snug and everything was aligned.

This was it. His life was effectively over. Some of the people in cryostorage had been there for 5,000 years since the Ship had launched, so there was a real chance he might never be thawed out. Even if he was, it would only happen because he had been dumped on a planet somewhere. He would never see the Ship again.

Zax had no regrets. He had done the right thing. He would do it all the same way again if given the chance. Well—everything except the arguments with Kalare. If he had it to do over, he would not give up a year of Kalare's friendship. His emotions had calmed during the process of getting dressed, but the memories of Kalare drove a fresh stream of tears from his eyes.

The cryotube creaked open and Zax focused on it with morbid fascination. He swiped at the tears and examined his new home through blurred vision. The only thing inside was a thin pad studded with contacts which would align with the suit's. The voice spoke again.

"Get into the tube."

What would happen if Zax refused? Would they send in the Marines to use overwhelming force and jam him into the cryotube, or would they flood the room with gas and eventually toss his unconscious body in like so much waste into a bin? It wasn't worth finding out, so he slid inside. The cover closed as Zax arranged his body and allowed the contacts on his suit to mate up with their partners on the pad. The electromagnets hummed and then the lid was secure and his body was locked into place. Finally—the hiss of gas.

This was it.

He had done his best to protect Mase and Kalare.

He hoped it was enough.

Goodbye, Mase.

Goodbye, Kal—

CHAPTER FORTY-TWO

You've always seemed ageless.

The Secretary's relatively puny head nodded in greeting as the connection went through. "Hello, Adan. How are things progressing?"

"Fine, Mr. Secretary. We've made great progress on the accommodations for your citizens since we last spoke. I've personally overseen the construction to ensure that everything is prepared according to plan."

Adan had successfully avoided conversations with the General Secretary for months, but it was finally time to bite the bullet and meet with the man. The work accomplished with the assistance of engineers the East provided to the mission had been truly phenomenal. It was all Adan could do to contain his excitement knowing he would be validating that work as soon as this meeting was complete. The Secretary spoke.

"We appreciate it, Adan. I have to say that, from everything I've heard, it's been a fantastic experience for everyone on the team to work with you. We greatly appreciate how you've welcomed us into your project."

"It's been my pleasure, Mr. Secretary. I'm quite pleased to know that we'll be able to take care of you and others from your society when we depart."

The words were easy for Adan because everything he had seen and planned for over the preceding months had made them absolutely true. The Secretary actually smiled for the first time in any of their discussions.

"I think that qualifies as the most surprising thing I've ever heard in my one hundred and sixty years."

Adan couldn't prevent himself from doing a double take, and the Secretary's smile transformed into laughter.

"What—did you legitimately not realize how old I was, Adan? I was already sixty when I was among the first of us who Uploaded. I've allowed my Pattern to age a little through the years that I've been General Secretary to give the appearance I was getting older, but I assumed everyone saw through that charade. Glad to see the effort paid off with at least one casual observer."

The man's words struck Adan momentarily speechless. The true age of the leader of the East must have been a matter of public record, but it had never occurred to him to seek out the information. The Chancellor was similarly ageless in his mind, but Adan knew full well her condition was thanks to the best genomic therapy that money and privilege could buy. Even with all of that, the most powerful woman in the West still faced the certainty of death within a handful of years following her one hundred and twentieth birthday. It really spun the game theory off into interesting directions when you imagined someone with the ability to literally wait out the death of his adversaries, and Adan discovered new appreciation for the General Secretary. He focused back on their conversation.

"My apologies, Mr. Secretary. But no, I was not aware of how old you are. You've always seemed ageless. I will admit to not having cared enough to pay attention to the fact that you truly are."

"No apologies necessary, Adan. Those of us in the East appreciate how much our lives differ from those of you in the West and how disorienting that can be. You've always associated me with this Pattern and that's fine, but ultimately it's nothing but the design for a uniform I slip into for my job. Sometimes I have different jobs and they require different uniforms. An ease with inhabiting various Skins is as natural for us after a hundred years as breathing is for you. I can hardly imagine what Patterns I might choose from at some point off in the future after you or your descendants have resettled me and my people. Perhaps we'll choose a glorious water planet and live as mermen. Regardless, we have you to thank for the opportunity to survive and we are grateful."

"Your gratitude, sir, is echoed in how all of us up here feel about the contributions of your team. In fact, I really should cut this call off now as I need to prepare for the final verification of their work."

"Thank you, Adan. I will look forward to shaking your hand soon."

No sooner was the connection cut than Adan was sprinting to their new transport system. The ability to get anywhere within the massive ship within a few seconds had really made his life far more efficient. He stepped out of the tube-shaped portal and bolted into the hangar. Markev waited along with a group of engineers, and he turned to Adan with a severe expression on his face.

"Good afternoon, sir. I would like to express one last time my sincere displeasure that you are allowing yourself to be a test monkey for this abomination of a device."

"Markev—I've been the first pilot for every single spacecraft, large and small, developed for this project. What evidence do you have from all the years you've known me that makes you think I'm going to change now?"

"I can appreciate that, sir, but this is the first time that being a pilot has required you to trust these freaks."

Adan grabbed his bodyguard by the shoulder and navigated the man a few meters away from the group of Eastern engineers who had watched their discussion with wide-eyed amazement. He looked up into his brawny assistant's eyes and pitched his voice low so only he could hear.

"I've asked you to trust me for many years now. Have I ever let you down or violated that trust?"

Markev paused but then shook his head.

"I've got to ask for that trust again here. I know you feel this has been the wrong direction for us. I know you feel I'm selling out our principles and beliefs for a handful of shiny trinkets. Please trust that I have a plan for doing what is best. For us. For humanity."

Markev nodded slightly and moved to walk away, but Adan reached back out and held him in place.

"No—I need you to say it."

"I trust you, Adan. I have no idea where this plan of yours might be leading, but I will trust you to get us there."

The bodyguard turned and walked back to the group of engineers. Adan paused for a deep breath. He knew where he wanted to go, and the path to getting there was becoming more and more clear with every passing day. This next test would be a key milestone in that journey, and he walked over to admire what the engineers had gathered around.

The fighter was a miracle of engineering. Capable of operating in both the vacuum of space and the atmosphere of a planet, its versatility was critical for a mothership which had severely limited space in which to store support craft. It could operate at nearly incomprehensible speeds for hours at a time thanks to the revolutionary engine powered by degenerate gas. It's only weakness came from an early design tradeoff to pack it with maximum firepower rather than include an FTL engine. All of this amazing technology was layered around a cockpit that could hold a pilot and a weapons system officer. It was this cockpit which Markev was so worked up about.

To support its versatility, the cockpit had been designed for two mission modes. Full life support systems allowed its crew to operate with or without spacesuits when flying manned missions. It was supporting unmanned missions where the real technological shift had occurred thanks to the engineers from the East. It would have been impossible to remotely pilot the craft effectively from afar due to the massive distances anticipated for space battles. Once the fighters traveled a few hundred thousand kilometers away from the ship, a second or more of communication latency would have left them vulnerable in a dogfight. The craft needed a crew on board, but a crew who could survive the life-crushing g-forces created by the acceleration and deceleration the machines were capable of.

For its first unmanned test flight, Adan had chosen to crew the fighter all by himself. He stripped out of his clothes and revealed the flight suit prototype he wore underneath. He pulled its hood over his head and adjusted it properly against his scalp. The metal contact points that were studded from the top of his skull to the base of his spine needed to be aligned just right to properly mate with the sensors built into his flight chair. Markev reached over at one point and assisted with those which were hardest for Adan to reach between his shoulder blades. Adan approached the chair and slid into it. With an audible click, his body locked into place and a red light next to Adan's hand began to flash. Markev leaned over his face.

"Are you ready, sir?"

Adan gave a thumbs up, and Markev shouted orders at the various engineers who were managing and monitoring the connection between the chair and the fighter. A few seconds later, the light next to his hand flipped from red to green.

This was the moment.

Adan pressed the button and all sensation was lost for a split second before it returned in a rush. He was sitting in the fighter. Its controls were arrayed around him. Outside the cockpit, a group of engineers encircled the chair in which the shell of his body currently resided. Markev stood to the side and wore a worried expression. Adan opened up a private communication channel to his bodyguard.

"Stop looking all gloomy like someone killed your puppy. I'm up in the cockpit now and I'm fine."

Markev looked up in his direction and Adan waved. There was no recognition in the man's eyes.

"If you say so, sir. The fighter looks just as empty to me as it did a minute ago."

Adan knew that statement to be true, but it provided an emotional jolt nonetheless. Sensors were feeding his consciousness visual input as if he was sitting in the cockpit, but he was not there. The only part of him that was actually on board the fighter was his mind. It had been transferred temporarily into the biological matrix housed in an armored core directly beneath the cockpit seats. It all made logical sense in the abstract, but it left him feeling short of breath if he focused on it too deeply.

It was time to fly.

"Markev—disconnect the transfer cable and button everything up. I'm ready to get out of here."

Adan's assistant issued orders and multiple engineers scurried around the fighter. Ninety seconds later, the giant stood in front of the craft and lifted both arms in a double-thumbs up signal. Adan moved to salute in return but caught himself with the realization yet again that he was not visible. He tapped the throttle and gently hovered the fighter ten meters off the deck. He pitched it forward and a few seconds later pierced the hangar's atmospheric force field and entered the vacuum of space. He increased acceleration until he was five kilometers away. He stopped and flipped the craft to face back toward the asteroid.

Bathed in Earthlight, his ship was sublimely beautiful. It was nearing completion with a skyline that rivaled the majesty of any city. One last tower which stood apart from the rest had a very different outward appearance and still crawled with construction equipment. Given it was for the East and therefore wouldn't actually be carrying people, it was no surprise that it matched none of the rest.

Adan's goal was nearly complete.

Their mission was almost ready to launch.

Only a few loose ends remained.

Adan pointed the fighter away from the ship, punched the throttle to maximum, and sped off into the void.

The Ship Series will continue with publication of Book Four and Book Five planned for 2017.

Thank you for reading. If you haven't already, I'd greatly appreciate if you could please write a quick review on Amazon for one or all of the books in the series. I've found it makes a **huge** difference for independent authors like me when prospective readers can learn more about a book from others.

If you want more from The Ship Series, please register on my website (theshipseries.com) or send an email to Zax@theshipseries.com. I will send you **a preview of Book Four**, offers for free bonus content, and updates on new releases. I also use my list to find readers who want early access to future books in exchange for providing feedback on initial drafts of the story. Never any spam - I promise.

Acknowledgments

Wow...what a year it has been since Landfall (Book One) and Revolution (Book Two) were published. I have been tremendously grateful for the way the books have been received and how they have been enjoyed by tens of thousands of readers. I had always assumed they might get seen by a few friends and maybe some random stragglers, so this response has been incredible.

There are a couple of key people to thank once again this time around who have been part of this journey across all three books. Owen Egerton remains an inspiration and someone with an eye for story that I find amazing. Stacey Swann provides fantastic editing and has helped this book be better both in its plot and its prose.

Claire Rushbrook is new to my team, but she had the thankless job of the final proofread. I am grateful for the many mistakes she caught before anyone reading this final draft ever saw them. Any that remain are most likely the fault of me making just those last few changes after her work was already done.

After I transitioned from being purely a writer and into the business side of independent authordom, a whole new crop of folks became involved who I would like to thank. First among these is Jonathan Paul Isaacs. Jon beat me to publication by a couple of years and I am wildly grateful for all of the advice and tips he has shared. It is nice to have a friend who has been a trailblazer and is willing to help you avoid some of the pitfalls that are out there. Jon has published three books in three different genres on Amazon - soon to be four. I've only read two of them so far, but he is a great writer so you can't go wrong with any of them.

Mark Dawson is an author with whom I am not personally connected, but to whom I nonetheless owe a debt of gratitude. Mark has created a community on Facebook for independent authors that has provided me with a wealth of knowledge and guidance around the business of being an author.

Lou Cadle and Jasper T. Scott are two authors who I have never met, but who reached out to me over the last year after reading Landfall. Each provided great feedback on the book and then were gracious enough to promote it to their audiences. Lou's *Gray* and Jasper's *Excelsior* are two fantastic reads. Ron Schrader is a third author who has been a wealth of assistance and information and I happily point you toward his *Humble Beginnings*.

Along with connecting with other authors now that I've published, the other huge change in my world as a writer has been the opportunity to connect with readers. It has been fantastic to interact with folks on Facebook and via email and I have received a ton of great feedback.

First among the folks I would like to thank is Mike Etheridge. Mike will always carry the distinction of being the first reader outside of friends/family who requested an autographed copy of Landfall. He shared some great feedback on the first two books, and then as an early reader of Book Three contributed to the final version of the story thanks to his thoughtful comments.

Mike was joined in my group of early readers by a number of other people to whom I am super grateful. Each of these readers participated in my early reader program and took the time to provide their thoughts about the book in advance of publication. They contributed in ways big and small to shaping what wound up on the page and I am lucky to have them reading my books. Andy, Bruce B., Jessica Bach, David Baxter, David Berkley, Chad Budd, Christian Bullow, Mark Burnett, Clint Burson, Rich Carmack, Ted Casey, Rob Colton, David Curno, Jeff Cushner, Scott Davis, Terence Drushel, Genti Duro, Marion Ekola, Benedict Fenner, Reid Ferguson, Art Ferris, Malin Fjallstrom-Hosack, Gideon Forder, Ward Freeman, John Geluk, John Graham, Tisha Havens, Michael Hekimian, Karen Herndon, Austin Isaacs, Todd Karvenek, Kory Kersavage, Thomas Kordusky, Mark Kurtz, Simon Lam, Michael Lee, Linda Lovely, Victor Maggiore, Kathy McIntyre, Thom Michaels, Paul Mockford, Eric Mohr, Brian Muldowney, Kyle Oathout, Gary Parks, David Patton, Brian Platt, Simon Ratcliffe, Maria Rogstadius, Harry Saul, Drew Schneider, Gavin Smart, Rick Smith, Randy Thomas, Sonya Villeda, Sharon Vreeland, Joshua Webb, Warren Whitley, Thomas Yamamoto, and Gregory Yeager.

If you would like to see your name on the above list next time, be sure to register at theshipseries.com or